TALES OF

THE BASTARD DRUNK

By

D.M. Woon

Mystery and Horror, LLC

Tarpon Springs, FL

Tales of The Bastard Drunk

Copyright © 2015 by Mystery and Horror, LLC

Author DM Woon
Sarah E. Glenn, Editor

First Trade Paperback Edition

ISBN- 978-0-9964209-1-4
(Mystery and Horror, LLC)

ISBN-10: 0996420916

Printed in USA by Mystery and Horror, LLC
Tarpon Springs, FL

For Alexia

If it hadn't been for you, this novel would've ended up in the growing pile of half-finished written ventures. You inspired me at a critical time, and cracked the whip until The Bastard Drunk was done. Your belief is monumental. This is for you.

TALES OF

THE BASTARD DRUNK

By

D.M. Woon

Mystery and Horror, LLC

Tarpon Springs, FL

Tales of The Bastard Drunk

Order of Play

- Act One -

- Act Two -

- Act Three -

There will be a brief interval at the end of Act Two

These tiny eyes watch
through threads of hair.
They never blink.
They only stare.
– notebook extract
Fitz Hanlon

The Travellers

A whole story in a split second; one instance, a thousand lives.

A woman falls against the wind, a man stands watching from the fire. A son cries out in pain, a mother lies in silent agony. A girl goes to sleep to escape life, a boy wakes to confront death. A woman sits beneath faltering light, two travellers walk through constant dark.

"It's no good, Fitz!" one traveller yelled into the raging storm. He stopped to adjust his rucksack and cast his gaze skyward, willing some form of light to show itself, but all he got in response was a face full of rain. He removed his glasses, lifted his red coat partially, and wiped them on the jumper he'd pulled over his chubby frame earlier that day. When he'd pushed them back on to the bridge of his nose, and sighed at the streaks of water that blurred his vision, he shouted to his fellow traveller once more, who had stopped a few paces in front. "I can't see, not for love nor money! Face it, we're lost; let's head back the way we came!"

There was a sudden stretch of lightning, swiftly followed by the sound of cracking thunder, which for one brief moment illuminated the travellers' path. They were quick to note that the road ended a short distance ahead, as did the houses that lined it on either side. A grassy verge sloped down to a wire fence, and a narrow footbridge that arced over to the next town. Two sodden planks of wood were sunken into the muddy bank, and a jagged board nailed between them displayed the words *NOW LEAVING*, but didn't say from where. That salient piece of information was lying face down on the railway tracks beneath the bridge, as the travellers soon discovered when they edged closer and peered down into the darkness, wondering what would greet them should they fall; and then the lightning lit up the sky once more to reveal the tracks.

"You go first, Paul!" Fitz shouted. He was ever so slightly taller than his friend, and in much better shape; his biceps strained against a tight white shirt beneath the blue coat he was wearing. "If she supports your weight, it'll be safe for me to cross!"

The bridge did indeed seem a little fragile as it swayed in the growing wind, with only a handrail made of rope either side of the wooden slats for support. Paul peered at Fitz from beneath the hood of his coat, eyes squinting through rain-lashed glasses. He ran a hand over his goatee beard as he smiled, and then laughed.

"Cheeky bugger! I might not be winning any slimmer of the year awards in the near future, but I still reckon my entire body weighs less than your fat head!"

Fitz smiled.

"Out the way, old man." He stepped past Paul, who was only six years his senior, and placed a firm foot on the first wooden slat of the bridge. He took hold of the sturdy rope handrail with both his hands and brought his hind leg forward in front of the other. He cautiously progressed; eyes fixed, as best as he could, upon his feet. The bridge continued to rock.

"Are we really risking our lives like this?" Paul cried. Fitz stopped, and glanced over his shoulder. Paul still stood on the grass; another flash of lightning and Fitz saw his look of concern. "This is insane. One minute, I'm running out of gas in my car; the next, I could be face down on the train tracks, and we're not even sure if we're heading the right way! I don't remember there being a bridge in the directions Kennedy sent us. It's late, Fitz; let's turn around. I'll make a phone call in the morning, tell them not to expect us. There'll be another convention–"

"No there won't! Not for me! Kennedy's been looking for any excuse to drop me from the wage bill for weeks now. I need this job, Paul. I can't miss this meeting."

"You put one foot wrong on that bridge and it won't just be a meeting you'll be missing. It'll be your daughter's childhood."

"You're a fine one to talk! Father of the fucking year over here; spare me the lecture, yeah? Are you coming or not? Because I'm crossing this bridge, with or without you."

"You'll never make it in time–"

"I can try!" Paul was taken aback by Fitz's roar, stunned by his angry expression. They stood still and looked at each other for a few seconds, in what would've been an awkward silence had it not been for the terrible weather and the squeaking of the bridge as it shook. "If Kennedy sees that I'm not there tomorrow, I'll be gone for sure. I need this job, Paul. Not just for me, but for Amy too." He turned and continued to tread carefully; he was halfway across when he felt Paul climb onto the bridge behind him, heard his footsteps *knock* on the wood and, wary of keeping a safe distance between them, Fitz quickened his pace.

Pangs of guilt were stabbing at him. He'd never raised his voice like that to Paul; he'd never had reason to. If it wasn't for him, he wouldn't have had a job at the company in the first place. He remembered the first time he'd met Kennedy; how Paul had *knock* knocked on his office door to introduce Fitz, and there Kennedy sat at his desk in a brown suit, and Paul stood in the doorway in a white collared shirt with a red tie and black trousers, and Fitz stood just behind him, his knees *knock* knocking together, wearing a slim-fit jumper and jeans. And all those times he'd let him crash on the

2

sofa, or given him a ride for the early shifts. How had Fitz repaid him so far? By missing two major deadlines in his first year and *knock* knocking up the girl from accounts. How had all this looked on his friend? Fitz made a face of repulsion; before long, he was safely on the other side, preparing his apology.

"Paul, I'm s…" He turned, and what he saw made his stomach churn.

The bridge was empty.

"Paul!" Images of his friend falling to a certain death plagued his mind. In a blind panic, Fitz stepped back on to the bridge, moving with real haste now, eyes frantically searching over the sides, yet seeing nothing through the veil of darkness. "Paul!"

"OK, I'm coming!"

Fitz looked up; another lightning flash, and he could just make out Paul's round figure, still stood on the grass, still in the other town. Fitz's mouth hung open. It didn't make any sense. Someone had been on that bridge with him, he was sure of it. Paul took hold of the rope and stepped slowly on to the wood; Fitz felt the bridge jerk slightly, just as it had a moment ago. Paul began edging closer, eyes clamped shut, hands firm on the rope, feet barely lifting from the wood as he made his way across, almost gliding over the surface. He was moving so slow, that Fitz had thought he'd stopped.

And then he did.

For he too heard a *knock*ing sound, approaching him, each knock more prominent than the last. And then a voice, female, wrought with despair, seemed to whisper softly in his ear.

Stay away.

"Who's there?" Paul shouted as he span around, but no reply came from the night. Fitz stared at him in confusion, and called his name, but Paul didn't hear; for another voice, male this time, and crackling with venom, was on the air, stealing his attention.

Come to me.

Paul turned once more, and saw no one but the faint outline of Fitz at the end of the bridge.

"Paul! What are you doing?"

Such a pretty voice–

"We need to keep moving!"

–let me taste–

"Paul!"

–bring that cunt to me!

A shrill scream exploded from nowhere, and Paul jolted forward. He tried to run, but his mind raced faster than his legs ever could; lacking composure, his movement was awkward, erratic, and he found himself stumbling across, barely upright, each stride more uncertain than the last. His footsteps were heavy; the wooden slats strained beneath him as he lumbered towards the end. He was almost there when the wood broke away under foot, and then Paul was falling, reaching out for something, *anything*, to save his life, and his hands met with the next slat, tried to grip but his palms slid, his fingers strained, tips whitened, bridge swayed as the wind whistled and the rain continued to fall. And then Fitz's hand reached through the hole and grabbed Paul, his other arm came down like the claw of an arcade machine and pulled him up. Paul closed his eyes in prayer.

"Please, not like this!"

You'll die by my hand tonight.

And it was as though Fitz found a new strength; he grunted as he heaved with all his might, and Paul held on for dear life as his body was guided up through the void. He could feel himself slipping from Fitz's grasp. As his legs rose higher, he swung them and found wood with his feet, pushed hard against it. Fitz stumbled backwards, dragged Paul with him; and together they fell panting to the grass bank of the other town.

Fitz gave Paul a shove and quickly jumped to his feet. Paul lay in a dirt puddle for a minute, trying to catch his breath; then Fitz spoke.

"What the fuck were you playing at?"

"The voices." Paul sat up. "You … you heard them, right?"

"I heard a scream; nothing more. Was probably just some kids playing around."

Paul began to shake his head, but words failed him, as Fitz turned to face the town. Silhouettes danced against the backdrop of night; a crescent moon made an appearance from behind the clouds to reveal a pockmarked strip of gravel lined with dilapidated buildings. Signs barely hung above doors loose on hinges, and scorch marks blackened storefronts that were otherwise white; gift shops mainly, but Fitz could see what was once a pharmacy, a post office, an off license. Refuse spilled from upturned bins that lay beneath boarded up windows, the sheets of wood smeared with graffiti. Debris decorated the pavement before them; an array of damaged odds and ends, and a bus shelter lay on its side, the rain pinging off its shattered shards of glass. "What is this place?"

And then he saw it; gleaming in blood red from a sheet of metal, attached to a pole cemented in the ground by the roadside: *KRAMUSVILLE*.

And not a *WELCOME TO* in sight…

The Finger Inn

"I don't believe it," Fitz said, his eyes fixated on the sign before him. He approached it cautiously, and ran his fingertips lightly over the letters as though he didn't believe they were real. Paul watched him silently; his breathing had almost returned to normal. Fitz turned to face him, then a smile spread wide across his face. "Paul, we made it!" He began fumbling through his jeans pocket as he dashed beneath a porch roof for shelter, before finally producing a map. Paul stared at him in disbelief.

"Are you out of your mind? This is a ghost town!" He stood and trudged over to Fitz; rain dribbled through cracks in ceramic tiles, but he was otherwise glad to be under cover.

"I know I've seen that name on here somewhere," Fitz replied, his eyes frantically roaming the unfolded sheet of paper in his hands, which he illuminated with his cell phone. Then he suddenly jabbed a finger hard into the map, his nail resting just below the name of a town. "There! You see? *Kramusville*. There's a train we can catch from here, right through to Riverbank Station. The hotel's a fifteen minute walk from there."

"And you know all this how?"

"Hey, don't sound so surprised. We 'non-drivers' need to get around too, you know." He folded the map up once more and shoved it back into his jeans pocket. "Your car breaking down wasn't such a bad thing after all." He playfully hit Paul's chest with the back of his hand, and stepped out into the rain.

"Well, I'm still going to give Kennedy a call." Paul tugged his mobile phone free from his coat pocket; with it, he produced a white envelope, which he hastily stuffed back inside, out of sight.

"What was that?" Fitz asked.

"Nothing."

"If it's nothing, why did you hide it so fast?" He shot Paul a look of ire. "Did they give you the Friermans dossier already? For fuck's sake, I told you they were looking to fire my arse!"

5

"Would you calm down? It's nothing to do with Friermans; it's another letter from Carol. Like I said, it's nothing."

"Have you opened it yet?"

"No."

"Then how do you know it's nothing? And why are you carrying it around with you if you have no intention of using it?"

"I could ask you the same question about that notebook of yours."

"You know I could fill that book up in a day if the right inspirations came."

"Then why do you never carry a pen?" Paul smiled as he stabbed a few buttons on his mobile phone, then held it to his ear. "Great," he said, frustration in his voice. "Straight to voicemail."

"So leave the guy a message."

"You know I don't talk to machines if I can help it, Fitz. I'm going to try calling the hotel." Paul pressed some more buttons, then held the phone to his ear again.

"Good evening, you're through to The Millerbank Hotel reception desk, this is Polly speaking, how may I help you?" Paul was so shocked by the sudden response that he almost forgot the words he'd intended to say.

"Hello ... Hi ... Yes, er, I need to speak to Mr. Scott Kennedy, I believe he's in Room 252."

"The Millerbank Hotel?"

"Yeah, he's leading the Amdion conference tomorrow afternoon, party of–"

"Hello, is anybody there?" Paul cleared his throat, and proceeded to raise his voice.

"Yes, my name is Paul Cooke, and I need to speak to Scott Ke–"

"God damn it!"

"Excuse me?"

"I'm getting tired of these fucking ghost calls! Do you think it's funny, harassing people like this? Get a life!" Paul's face was almost the same colour as his coat.

"There's no need to lose your head, lady!" he shouted furiously. "Now, I need to speak to my boss! Can you do that for me?"

"Stop calling here, you freak!" The line went dead.

"Damn it!" Paul punched the screen of his mobile phone. Fitz was laughing.

"Trouble with the line?"

"Either that or some chick just got her period. I'm going to send Brian a text; at least they'll know where to look for our bodies." He stepped out next to Fitz. "So, where do we find this train of ours?" Fitz pointed to a lamppost a short distance ahead, to which was attached a metal sign that read *St. Arthur's Walk*, barely readable by the lamp's dim light. The sign pointed off to the left, and without

6

another word between them, the travellers began to walk.

The buildings they passed once they turned the corner were in much better condition than those Kramusville had already offered them, though they still looked in desperate need of some tender loving care. These buildings were evidently houses; all had numbered front doors crying out for a lick of paint, and windows that looked so thin they may as well have been made from cellophane. Only a few of the houses had vehicles parked outside, though they hardly appeared roadworthy, with punctured tyres and shattered windscreens.

"Do you think people live here?" Paul asked. Fitz responded with a nod, eyes locked on an upstairs window as he passed. Paul followed his gaze, and saw a young boy waving down at them. Just as quickly as Paul had seen him, his mother appeared from behind, her face contorted with fear; she pulled the child away from the window, and drew the curtains shut.

The rain only worsened as they continued down the road, which showed no signs of ending as it emerged from the gloom before them, until it suddenly came to a T-junction. Paul and Fitz stopped to survey their options; no signs informed them of which way to turn. The road on the left seemed to lead to a cul-de-sac, so after brief deliberation they turned right, and found themselves passing a large supermarket. Though the exterior was as dark as every other building they'd seen, some lights appeared to be on inside, dim glows faintly visible through the darkness beyond the sliding doors, casting little luminosity on the car park that stood before it, empty except for one vehicle parked near the entrance.

"Shall we stop and ask for directions?" Paul suggested. Fitz shook his head.

"It's this way, it has to be." Figures seemed to be loading shopping bags into the rear of the car. "It's fucking zombies that shop at this time of night; I doubt they could tell us shit anyway." They continued on their way, treading carefully as the road sloped downwards and veered left, past an apartment building with stairs on the outside, above which a neon arrow flickered the letters *BJs*, and pointed towards a door that the stairs led down to. Fitz nudged Paul as they looked at the sign. "I could do with one of those right now," he said with a smile.

"If you can get us on this train and out of this weather within the next thirty seconds, I might just go down on you myself!" Before long, their laughter had been drowned out by the howling wind, and as they strained their eyes with every step they took, finally they could just make out their destination a little way ahead. The nearer they drew, the more evident the words *ST. ARTHUR'S WALK TRAIN STATION* became; painted in white above a ticket booth that stood before the platforms, visible by the lights of a nearby pub.

"What did I tell you?" Fitz shouted, and after exchanging glances, they quickened their pace towards the ticket booth. However, it soon became clear that nobody was inside; no face peered out at them from behind the grubby glass screen.

"Now what?" Paul asked.

"Now we wait for our train."

"Fitz, there's nobody here. This station probably isn't even in service anymore."

"I checked public transport routes!" Fitz snapped defensively. "Why would they give me a train that doesn't run?"

"So what time is our train then?"

Fitz didn't reply immediately. "I'm not sure. I don't remember."

Paul looked at him as best he could through his rain-struck lenses, and saw a tormented expression. "I don't remember," Fitz repeated, his head dropping. Paul stared up at the pub.

"*The Finger Inn*," he read aloud. "Lights are on; do you think anybody's home?" Fitz lifted his head once more. Then without a moment's hesitation, he darted for the inn. Paul smiled, and followed as fast as his weary legs would allow.

At first, the door didn't seem to want to budge, but as Paul rushed to get out of the rain, he fell into his companion; the weight of the two men saw the door tearing open, and they stumbled inside.

"Hello?" Fitz called, as the door shuddered shut behind them. Though the interior was dimly lit, they would've been forgiven for mistaking that the pub was closed. It was dark and deserted inside, and the bar looked like it hadn't been tended for a long time. Chandeliers hung from the high ceiling, though no light came from them. Candles burned faintly in holders along walls otherwise empty; there were no symptoms that paint had ever graced their surface, and they were decorated with stains instead of artwork. Tables and stools were unevenly scattered on the large wooden floor, gathering dust instead of beverage spills. A jukebox stood in the far corner, or a *JKBX* if the remaining flickering bulbs were to be believed; doors to the right of it led off to the toilets, though the *Laydies* were out of order, while the *Jents* looked in desperate need of affection.

"Can I help you, boys?"

Paul and Fitz jumped at the sound of a croaked voice, heavy with a rural inflection. From the shadows behind the bar emerged a tall, thin man, cleaning a dirt-filthy glass with a tea towel ridden with moth bites and burns. He wore dark, black trousers and a dull grey shirt that seemed as though it was once a bright white. A black bow tie complimented his attire; a pair of lime green kitchen gloves, however, did not. The barman smiled; a near toothless grin, except for an incisor that jutted out awkwardly from his bottom gum. His hair was surprisingly well kept, slicked back and blacker than the night sky outside. He had one beady brown eye focused on them, and the other, evidently false, was rolled to the top of the socket. A long and crooked nose wormed down his weathered face and pointed at them, before the barman's smile faded and he stopped smudging grime round the glass in his hand.

"Are ya a couple o' imbeciles or somethin'?" the barman shouted suddenly. "I asked you boys a question. I see that ya got tongues in them heads o' yours, so I expect an answer!"

"What time does the train pass through here?" Fitz said in a hurry. The barman's smile reappeared.

"Depends which way yer traversin', young fellas," he replied.

"We need to get to The Millerbank Hotel. It's right near–"

"I know where it's right near, boy! Don't think that you know more 'bout this town than I do." There was an awkward silence, even more unnerving than the one that met them when they entered the inn. The rain grew fiercer still, slammed against the window with the force of a fist, and it surprised the travellers that the glass did not shatter upon impact. "Trains are every half hour." Paul and Fitz turned to walk. "Monday through Friday, that is." The barman stabbed a thin, crooked finger at the calendar by the bar. "Last time I checked, today is Saturday."

"How often do they run at weekends?"

"Every hour. Tickets are usually a li'l pricier, but they won't cost ya a penny since our Maureen had a seizure an' died; ain't ya in luck?" The travellers exchanged a perplexed glance. "The westbound service usually gets to St. Arthur's Walk at seven minutes past." Both men checked the clock above the bar. It had just gone past eleven.

"Thanks!" Fitz shouted, as he jerked the door open and headed towards the station.

"See you later!" Paul called as he followed, and the door slammed shut. The barman smiled.

"Sooner than you think, Four Eyes. Sooner than you think."

Twenty-five minutes had passed before Paul turned to Fitz as they stood on the platform, and questioned the whereabouts of their train.

"How the fuck am I supposed to know?" Fitz replied. "You heard the man the same as I did. Seven minutes past the hour." He glanced at the clock perched above the platform, and cursed loudly into the wailing wind.

"Come on," Paul said, "let's head back to the pub." They trudged in silence from the platform, past the empty ticket booth and down the short gravel pathway to The Finger Inn. Fitz shoved the door fiercely, this time swinging it open without difficulty. The barman stood behind the bar, still pushing his tea towel around the glass, as though he hadn't moved an inch since the travellers had left his pub.

"Why'd you lie to us about the trains?" Fitz growled, storming across the floor and pounding his fist on the bar; dust rose and settled in new formations.

"Case you din't notice 'em, Muscle Man, I gots me some ears, an' they work jus' fine. There's no need to be raisin' that voice o' yours." Fitz grabbed the barman by the scruff of his shirt and pulled him close.

"Fitz, let go!" Paul yelled, taking hold of his friend's arm.

"I'd listen to Four Eyes if I was you," the barman said calmly. Fitz glared at him for a moment, then tore his hand away. "I thought as much," the barman said, straightening up. "Now, what seems to be the nature o' your predicament?"

"You told us that the trains come through here at seven minutes past the hour," Paul said, in a far calmer tone than Fitz had managed.

"They do," the barman replied. "But ain't no train comin' through here after eleven at night. You boys missed the last one over an hour ago."

"And you didn't think to tell us that before?" Fitz shouted.

"See now, you asked me how often the trains run, an' I toldya. If yer wanted to know when the last train *was*, ya shoulda amended your enquiry." The barman let out a little laugh.

"Fuck you."

"Do you kiss your mother with that mouth?"

"So what do we do now?" Paul interjected before Fitz could respond. The barman eyed him curiously with a smile.

"Way I see it is, you an' your vulgar friend can either step outside in the pourin' rain, wait until the 07:07 pulls in, freeze those Lord forsaken behinds off; or ya can pull up a stool an' keep warm an' dry."

"Get fucked!" Fitz spat, and he turned to face the door, but Paul stood in his way.

"I don't see what other choice we have, Fitz. Either way we're going to have to wait until morning for our train; better done in the warmth, don't you reckon? Besides, we'll catch our deaths out there. Pull up a chair and chill out, for God's sake." Paul grabbed a stool at the bar and sat down; the barman smiled.

"Fine." Fitz sat down at the nearest table. "You just keep that freak away from me, or I won't be accountable for my actions."

"What'll it be?"

"I'll just take a glass of water, thanks."

"An' for Muscle Man?"

"I don't want anything from you."

The barman glowered suddenly.

"Now boys, I only entertain payin' customers."

His scowl was fixed, so Paul hastily changed his mind to keep the peace.

"We'll take two of your finest ales. Please." The barman's smile returned once more, and he proceeded to pour two pint glasses to the brim with ale. Paul took a note from his wallet, pocketed his change and took the drinks over to the table Fitz had sat at.

"So what now? We just sit here for the next eight hours and drink?"

"I gots a spare bedroom upstairs if ya need to get your heads down."

Fitz stood up angrily.

"I don't care if *ya* got Ange-*fuckin'*-lina up there ready to suck my dick–"

"Would you keep the fuckin' noise down?" came a booming voice from the back of the pub. Paul and Fitz turned, and saw for the first time that a man sat near the jukebox. It was too dark to see him properly, but there was no denying that his presence unnerved the travellers. Paul gulped silently to himself, and Fitz sat back down.

"Is there gonna be a problem here, Riley?" The man's voice oozed with a heavy drawl: American, Southern.

The barman smiled at his guests.

"I don't think so," he replied. "Mr. Muscle Man here seems to get the message." Then he lowered his voice to address only the travellers. "You boys jus' disturbed The Bastard Drunk. If ya plan on spendin' the night here, I suggest you make it up to him. Could even be worth your while."

"Excuse me?" Paul asked. The barman leaned closer towards them.

"Buy The Bastard a brandy, an' he might jus' tell you a tale 'bout this town." Paul glanced at Fitz, seemed to pause for a few seconds, and they just looked at each other as though trying to read minds, before Paul placed a hand on his wallet once more, and Fitz stared at him in disbelief.

"You're not really going to buy him a drink, are you?"

"If it'll give us something to pass the time with," Paul replied, before nodding at the barman. "Besides, it might be nice to know about the place we're staying in. Even if it is just for one night." In exchange for another note, Paul received a small glass of brandy and an even smaller amount of change.

"The guy screams at a couple of strangers from the back of an empty bar, and you think it's wise to go and entertain him?"

"He's probably just a lonely old man. I bet he'd appreciate the company."

"I reckon he'd appreciate it more if we stayed the hell away from him. The guy is lonely for a reason. There's plenty of empty stools down here, and yet he chooses to sit up back in the shadows. He isn't looking for conversation–"

"So let's take the conversation to him."

"What makes you think he's even going to talk?"

"You heard the barman; buy him a drink, and he'll tell us a story."

"O' course, ya could always exchange pleasantries with me instead if that's your preference," the barman interrupted with a grin. "I can be quite the point o' interest." Paul looked at Fitz knowingly, as Fitz shot the barman a disapproving look.

"Your choice, Fitz," he said, taking a sip of his ale and licking his lips in satisfaction. Fitz picked up his drink and stood; the barman continued to smile as Paul led the way towards the rear of the pub.

"So we're just going to fund some stranger's alcohol addiction for the next eight hours?" Fitz asked as they approached the figure sat in the shadows.

"Depends. If his stories are as bad as my ex-wife's, this will be the only drop of brandy this *Bastard* gets from me." Paul smiled, and Fitz couldn't help but lighten up a little bit.

The Bastard Drunk

Though darkness still obscured him, and his head tilted down towards his glass, Paul and Fitz still felt sure The Bastard's gaze was cast upon them as they neared, but he didn't look up to acknowledge them properly until Paul placed his peace offering on the table and cleared his throat. The Bastard's head turned slowly, and by candlelight they saw him now. His hair, grey and shaggy, fell beside a worn and wrinkled face; eyes, small and brown, peered between strands that dangled before them. There was a long, thin cut beneath his right eye, and he had what Paul would refer to as a "drinker's nose," large and red, the touches of rosacea. A rough grey goatee beard framed his thin pale lips, and stray hairs stretched across his cheeks and down his neck. He looked in good need of a wash, as did the long grey coat that he wore buttoned up to his chest. The Bastard nodded towards the drink that Paul had set beside him.

"The fuck is this?" As he spoke, he revealed more teeth than the barman, but the colourless stumps still fell considerably short of a full set. Fitz recoiled at the scent of his stale breath.

"Brandy," Paul replied, sliding it closer to The Bastard's hand. "Courtesy of the troublemakers." The Bastard watched as the glass skated across the wooden table top towards him, stopping just short of his right hand, and then he eyeballed Paul curiously.

"What did Riley tell you?" he asked, his eyes narrowing.

"Excuse me?"

"You don't sidle up to a stranger in a bar and present him with his choice o' poison without the knowledge o' what he's drinkin'. And if the next words outta your mouth don't profess your psychic abilities, they best reveal what Riley told you."

"Just that you could let us know a thing or two about this place."

"Is that so?" The Bastard replied. He leaned back in his chair, the wood creaking as his slender frame shifted. "And there was me thinkin' you wanted my cock up your ass." He laughed to himself, but when Paul joined in, he stopped abruptly. "Tell me; are you a scholar or a fool?"

"Excuse me?"

"Lesser men have learned not to trust the word o' Riley Creeper. Let me see; did he tell you that I'm *The Bastard Drunk*, and that I'll spill the deepest darkest secrets o' Kramusville if you ply me with alcohol?"

"That's about right."

"And you cocksuckers came right on over with a glass o' brandy and your hearts full o' hope, dincha? Well, bless your fuckin' cotton ones. I'm just glad Riley didn't tell you I'd chew the crap from your ass hair. The sight o' your faces is bad enough–"

"Is your name The Bastard Drunk or not?" Fitz spat suddenly. The Bastard slowly turned to face him, his face etched with irritation.

"*Is my name The Bastard Drunk?* Were my parents married when I was born? No. Do I drink myself into a stupor on a regular basis? Hell yeah I do. *Is my name The Bastard Drunk?* Course it fuckin' ain't! You ever met a man by the name o' *The* before? Didn't think so; what a stupid thing to ask! But have the circumstances surroundin' my birth, and my daily consumption o' alcohol, led some to label me The Bastard Drunk over the years? I believe so, yeah. But you two fucks don't know me well enough to address me by that moniker. And I don't know *you* well enough to be on a first name basis."

"I'm Paul. This is Fitz." The Bastard leapt to his feet and grabbed Paul by the scruff of the neck. His fragile appearance belied a strength the travellers did not think possible; Paul was frozen with fear, and Fitz was simply stunned by The Bastard's swift movement.

"You think tellin' me your God damn names is gonna lessen the severity o' the mess you find yourselves in?" Fitz snapped into life, and with great difficulty he separated the pair of them. The Bastard staggered back a step, before squaring up to Fitz. There was very little difference in height between them, and for a moment they just stood toe to toe, glaring into each other's eyes, trying to intimidate, but both too stubborn to back down that neither man moved.

"Come on, Fitz," Paul said. He had straightened his coat and was rubbing his throat, red marks already visible from The Bastard's firm grasp. "Let's find our own table. You were right; this guy obviously doesn't want any attention."

"Take heed o' what your friend is sayin'," The Bastard growled. "Problem child like yourself in a strange town like this; you need attention like a cripple needs a flight o' stairs." He stepped back and grabbed the glass of brandy from the table, brought it up to his lips and threw the liquid past his gums in one. Fitz continued to stare at him, though his expression was now one of disbelief.

14

"You drank the drink."

The Bastard slammed the glass down and wiped his beard with the back of his hand.

"Well observed," he replied. "What else was I gonna do with it? Dip my junk in to see if it'll float?"

"Leave it, Fitz–" Paul started.

"Bullshit! The old man just drank the brandy you bought him. He owes us a fucking story now whether he likes it or not." The Bastard narrowed his eyes once more.

"Come again?"

"*Buy The Bastard a brandy, an' he might jus' tell you a tale 'bout this town,*" Fitz said, repeating Riley's words in an exaggerated accent.

The Bastard snorted.

"I believe the operative word in that sentence o' yours is *might*. There ain't nothin' legally bindin' about it."

"Come now, Hanson," came Riley's voice from the bar. All eyes turned to see that he was still wiping glasses with his tattered rag. "These boys did go to all the trouble o' buyin' you a drink; what say you give 'em a li'l story or two for their efforts?" Before The Bastard could respond, Riley suddenly stopped cleaning, and he seemed to darken somewhat. "Unless you want me to tell 'em a tale o' my own," he added, with unnerving sincerity in his voice. The Bastard's eyes widened momentarily, and then he angrily dropped into his seat.

"Fine," he spat. "One brandy gets you one tale; I ain't a fuckin' charity case." Fitz and Paul shared a brief smile, before pulling up chairs and sitting opposite their new acquaintance.

"So what have you got in store for us, Hanson?" Paul asked, and The Bastard looked like he was fit to tear the man's head clean from his shoulders.

"If you dare to call me by the name my mother bestowed upon me one more time, I swear to God, I will hurt you. In ways you've never imagined possible. Do I make myself clear?" Paul nodded, and sipped on his ale. "I've got tales about this place that could evoke any emotion from within you two cocksuckers. I could make you laugh, but I don't feel like bein' funny. I could make you feel all warm inside, or I could chill you to the bone. I could even make you cry if I wanted to, and I'm mighty tempted, 'cause I bet your stupid little fuck faces would look even dumber with tears for Momma rollin' down your cheeks."

"Are you going to tell us a tale, or just insult us?" Fitz interrupted.

"Both; if I have it my way. And I *will* have it my way. I'm the one who will be tellin' the tale after all."

"So what's the tale about?" Paul asked.

The Bastard leaned back in his chair, and sported a wry grin for a split second.

"Why don't you decide that for yourselves?"

"For fuck's sake, just tell us about our train," Fitz said hastily. The Bastard looked at him like he was nothing more than dog mess he'd trodden in.

"*Your train?* You want a story about a train?"

"I know, I'm sorry," Fitz replied. "Stupid thing to ask, right?"

"You're damn right it's a stupid thing to ask!" The Bastard slammed his fist down on the table; droplets of alcohol sloshed up the inside of the travellers' glasses and splashed out on to the wood.

"Maybe you could suggest a subject–" Paul started, but The Bastard jerked his head fiercely so that he was now staring at him instead of Fitz.

"You'll get your train story," he growled quietly, and then he scraped his chair closer to the table and motioned for the travellers to do the same.

"I thought it was a stupid idea?" Fitz asked testily. "Why the sudden change of heart?" The Bastard ran fingers through his greasy hair, and glowered at Fitz once more.

"Stupid, yes. But it's not my change o' heart that should concern you; it's your own! 'Cause once you hear the tale o' pretty Polly Whitmore, you might just think twice about catchin' *your* train come mornin' light."

Tale 1

$P_{retty} \; P_{olly}$

1

It takes a little longer than thirty minutes to arrive at Riverbank Station from St. Arnold's Walk.

Pretty little Polly Whitmore knew that only too well. She'd taken the train to work for as long as she could care to remember, catchin' the 08:07 every mornin', and arrivin' at Riverbank Station thirteen stops later at twenty minutes to nine. By the time she walked to The Millerbank Hotel, where she was employed as a receptionist, her shift would be just about ready to start. And then, when the workin' day was done, Polly would walk back to the station and take the train home again. Sometimes, she was lucky enough to catch the 17:21 service; but, more often than not, she would have to hang around for the 17:51, and arrive at St Arnold's Walk a little after twenty past the hour. She'd be home warmin' her feet by the fire long before the clock chimed seven times.

But on the night in which this tale is set, Polly had to work herself some overtime.

Why?

You don't question how I know her daily routine, but you wanna know *why* she didn't get outta work 'til late? I dunno, maybe Erin the evenin' receptionist was gettin' her tubes tied, do I look like a fuckin' psychic to you?

All I know is, by the time Polly Whitmore made it to Riverbank Station, the last train was just pullin' in. Polly slides a note into the booth, snatches her ticket, doesn't even take her change she's in such a hurry. Shouts a breathless thanks, rushes her fine ass down the steps and jumps on the train just as the doors are about to snap shut.

She glances down the carriage; an old guy is fast asleep several rows down, his head restin' back on the window. Someone else is sat a little further away. They're wearin' a long black jacket with the hood pulled over their head, concealin' their face; the shape o' their body tells Polly that it's a woman, though she can't be too sure.

She sinks into the nearest seat, sighs louder than she intends to, laughs silently to herself. Her stomach growls, cries out for that lasagne in the freezer, and Polly rests her hand on her abdomen as if to silence it. She feels her mobile phone in her pocket, so she pulls it out and sees that her boyfriend Chris has sent her a text message. *Probably somethin' smutty, if my knowledge o' that prick serves me right. He used to work the till at the butcher's shop, and whenever a lady went in to buy some goods, he'd communicate in innuendo with a wink and the smile o' a fuckin' pervert; asked my Emily if she'd like his sausage between her buns once. She said she'd like to pound his meat instead.*

With a fuckin' tenderiser. God rest her soul.

Anyways, whatever Chris' text said, it made Polly giggle like a naughty schoolgirl. But then her smile fades when she notices a second text message, this one from her mother. Somethin' along the lines o': *We need to talk. I'm coming over tomorrow. I love you.* Polly's smile returns; she's waited so long to read that text. She finds *Chris* in her contact list and makes a call. It doesn't even ring, it just goes straight to voicemail, and Polly realises the train has gone underground en route to the next station.

"Hey Chris, I just got your message, sorry but I'm not taking any pictures tonight. I'm on the train home, just worked the longest shift ever, Erin called in sick so I had to stay until late. So, I've got some bad news. We're going to have to cancel our dinner plans tomorrow night. Mom has decided that she's coming over to my place to talk things through. Call me crazy, but this just might be the talk that puts all bad feelings behind us, and I don't want to pass that opportunity up. I'll make it up to you, I promise. I love you."

She can't do both, right? No protagonist can ever be in two places at once. Polly ends the call, remembers the argument she had with her mom last November, the nights she cried herself to sleep over the horrible words they'd exchanged. The way Chris had pulled her through, made her see that it wasn't her fault; and then she damn near cries at the thought o' her dear old mother sittin' in her favourite armchair, the arthritis slowly consumin' her body, wonderin' if she'll ever see her daughter again; swallows her pride, finds the courage to pick up the phone and leave a message. Polly pinches her eyes shut tight; fuck, she missed her mother. Needed her more than ever recently, what with the miscarriage and all.

Get to the point?

Are you fuckin' serious? You boys paid an extortionate amount for that brandy; Riley knows his prices are through the roof, but as long as he's gettin' custom, does it look like he gives a fuck? And I'm sittin' here, outta the kindness o' my heart, makin' sure you get your money's worth, and you want me to fast forward to the good part? Fuck you! You'll do well to remember that I'm the one tellin' this story. And if the narrative devices that I choose to employ aren't to your likin', you don't need my permission to be excused from the table. You're more than welcome to go fuck yourself. This is all necessary exposition. You don't care enough about Polly Whitmore for me to kill her off in spectacular fashion just yet. I want you to *know* her before she dies. Only then can this tale have the desired effect.

The train carries on its journey, bobbin' and bouncin' down the track like a snake with the shakes. A couple o' times, Polly's firm behind leaves the seat, and she panics briefly.

You know when your brain does that to you? Tells you that your train ride isn't usually this erratic, convinces you that some terrorist has emptied a handgun into your driver and is about to waste everybody on board. You start to think o' all your loved ones, tunin' in to the news channel and hearin' about a train crash, anguished faces realisin' the possibility that you mighta been on that train, the frantic diallin' o' your mobile number, tremblin' lips leavin' heartfelt messages; flash-forward to your funeral, family members who haven't seen each other in years, united to grieve at your passin', and you're so caught up in that image that for a moment you believe you are actually dead. I've seen my headstone countless times, witnessed loved ones lay flowers at my grave; but then I wake up right at this very table, and decide I've had enough to drink for one night. There's solace in that instance; just like when the train slows down as it approaches the next station, and eases to a stop beside the platform. Polly's heart quits racin' as the doors slide open, and no one suspicious lookin' enters the carriage.

I love that phrase. *Suspicious lookin'*. Makes you wonder what others define as *suspicious*, doesn't it? Is it shifty eyes? A peculiar scar? The generosity o' buyin' a stranger a drink? I tell you what Polly found *suspicious lookin'*. The figure wearin' the long black coat with the hood up. Hadn't budged an inch. The doors slide shut. The train rolls on.

They go above ground; the sky's been painted an eerie shade o' black, the moon is swallowed whole somewhere up there, and if it hadn't been for the sudden lashin' o' rain against the window, Polly woulda been forgiven for thinkin' she was still in a tunnel. The water smashin' into the pane startles her, and she loses herself for a moment in the movement o' the droplets, slidin' down the glass and formin' as one at the bottom. For some reason, it reminds her o' the first time she ever saw snow. Those individual elements fallin' gracefully, and congregatin' before her very eyes. Daddy helped her build a snowman. Promised he'd never let it fade away. Daddy often made promises he couldn't keep. Said he'd always love Polly and her mother. Walked out on 'em both three weeks shy o' her seventh birthday. It had snowed that evenin', too. Polly made her own snowman, in the hope it'd bring her father back. It didn't work. Polly never saw Daddy ever again. And she certainly never made another snowman.

But there'd be times in years to come when she would hear her daddy's voice sayin' her name, callin' to her from the foot o' the staircase, and Polly would throw down her dolls and go rushin' downstairs, only to be greeted by the sight o' her mother consolin' herself with another bottle o' whiskey. Unopened bottles o' pills, Mommy couldn't do it, not now, not yet, not with Pretty Polly around.

And then there is it again, her name, creepin' through the air and curlin' up inside her ears; once more, with greater prominence this time, and Polly is unsure if it is her imagination, or if she has heard it for real, right there, on the train.

You ever heard your own name on the wind before? That overwhelmin' sense o' fear and confusion when you turn to find nobody there? Well, that's what Polly felt in that carriage. Her eyes are dartin' everywhere for a sign, but findin' none. Just an old guy fast asleep, and a hooded figure that still hasn't moved. The lights start flickerin' as the train disappears underground once more; then they blink out altogether, and Polly is plunged into darkness.

6

Polly had been scared o' the dark for as long as she could care to remember. For a moment, her mind goes blank and she can't recall why. She pictures herself in a very dark place; she knows it happened a long time before she was pickin' out baby names for a child she'd never hold, but for some reason the metaphorical outweighs the literal, and she hears herself sayin' "Rosa."

"Any particular reason?" Alexia asks, sippin' her chai latte and motionin' to the waiter with her right hand.

"It's my mother's name," Polly replies with a vacant smile. Alexia frowns.

"I didn't think you and your mother got along?"

"That doesn't mean I've stopped loving her. I never will." She places her hands on her stomach. "I want her to be a part of this baby's life; but she has to want that too. And for that to happen, she will apologise for what she said at Dad's funeral, and concede that she wants to be a part of *my* life again." Alexia rests a comfortin' hand on Polly's forearm and smiles.

"I realise now just how long I have missed you for. Years have been stolen from our friendship, and yet they feel like only months at most. Every time you crossed my mind at the hostel, I told myself that we'd see each other soon, and that nothing would have changed. Today, I looked across the table and saw a skinny white girl with pigtails, burdened with a broken home, bullied by older girls, locked in broom cupboards, friend of a rebel outcast. Yet minutes later I see a beautiful young woman with a voluptuous figure, perfect blonde hair, and seductive caramel eyes that reveal no signs of the pain she once adhered to. And me? What have I become?"

"A Godmother." And Polly sees Alexia's face light up at the prospect o' belongin' once again. Her eyes grow wide in delight; but then the darkest reaches o' Polly's mind begin to distort that memory. Pupils dilate and consume Alexia's face, and all Polly sees is black, and all Polly hears is laughter, cruel laughter, from behind the broom cupboard door; and she remembers then just why she is scared o' the fuckin' dark.

Snap outta it! She wills herself awake, she is back now, on the train, in the carriage, but the laughter does not cease, it gets louder, and Polly realises then it is real, so real, and that evil is there with her. Fear grips her tight, like a noose about the neck, and she fumbles with her mobile phone, tries to illuminate all before her, only succeeds in castin' faint shadows, panics her further. The lights flash overhead, make her jump, and then they come to life as the laughter dies, and Polly is breathless, frozen, stunned to see that the scene is not unlike before. Old man fast asleep, his chin now restin' on his chest. And hooded figure, still ominously present at the end.

7

St. Arnold's Walk is still three stops away, but Polly decides she's had quite enough o' this particular train ride, and figures she can get off at Mayuri Avenue and walk the rest o' the way home, regardless o' the rain pissin' down. Gettin' wet had always proven to be a far more pleasant experience than havin' the shit scared outta her. Cautiously she stands, silently wipes her face with the palm o' her hand, steps carefully towards the doors, doesn't wanna attract attention. Sees the platform drawin' closer, wants to hear a familiar voice upon leavin' the train, finds *Mom* in her contact list and prepares to hit the dial key.

And then the train rocks violently; Polly goes stumblin' forwards, and the old guy's head falls back onto the window, and all Polly sees is this big fuckin' void where his throat should be. She screams and steps away. The wound was so clean! There wasn't even a drop o' blood on the guy's shirt, never mind his skin. Polly is hysterical; the hooded figure starts laughin', the same malicious cackle, and for the first time Polly catches sight o' their face. She had been right; it was a woman.

Well, as woman as an apparition can be.

Bright blue eyes stare out maniacally beneath a lightnin' white fringe barely visible behind the hood. Lips, ruby red, part as the laugh becomes an almighty roar, barin' jagged teeth still drippin' with blood; the cleanliness o' the wound becomes apparently clear.

"I never leave a drop," the phantom snarls. And then before Polly's eyes, she twists with such vehemence that she becomes a smudge, and then disappears altogether. Polly's mouth hangs open, but no sound musters the courage to come out. The train stops at Mayuri Avenue.

"Hello?"

A voice crackles from the phone in Polly's tremblin' hands, and she glances down to see that she musta hit the button and called Mom. Polly raises the phone to her ear.

"Hello? Polly, I do hope you can hear me. I made a terrible mistake the day of your father's funeral. Of course you weren't to blame for him leaving us. I miss you so much." And she was cryin' now. "I love you with all my heart, dear. Please find it within to forgive me."

"Mom," Polly whispers through tears. She turns to face the doors as they slide open. "I–" And then this ghostly fist slams into her face without warnin', sends her soarin' through the air. Her teeth shatter upon impact, mouth quickly fills with blood as shredded gums leak, and as her body lands with a thud at the other end o' the carriage, a fountain o' vibrant red spurts into the air as she fights for breath. Polly's a fuckin' mess; tears slidin' into snot slidin' into bloodied spit. She has enough time to weakly claw broken teeth from her mouth, before a foot connects with her jaw with all the force o' a sledgehammer. Her screams o' agony do little to conceal the sound o' breakin' bone that echoes in her ears.

She is dragged up by her hair, as though she weighs nothin' at all, a mere marionette in a ventriloquist's hands. Her feet, several inches from the floor, dangle almost lifelessly as she whispers one final plea; and then in one swift motion, she's slammed into the carriage wall. Spine collides with metal at an alarmin' pace, splinters like a twig. Polly drops to the floor, as good as dead, and this woman reappears, mutterin' "I never leave a drop" obsessively, starts suckin' up pools o' blood from all over the carriage, laughin' maniacally all the while. And Polly, well, she still has this brain workin' inside o' her, bless, she sees an opportunity. She starts spittin' blood everywhere, knowin' the spook wouldn't be able to resist cleanin' up before makin' certain that Polly is dead. She waits for the right time to start crawlin' with all her might towards the doors. And she can smell the night air, she can almost taste freedom, hands touch down on cold, wet concrete, and just as she dares dream that she's made it, she feels a firm hand wrap around her ankle.

Fingernails scratch and break as she tries to dig them into the solid surface while bein' pulled back on board. She can only kick her feet weakly, it's no use, she succumbs. Her mother's voice still crackles in her palm, tormented by the sound o' her beloved daughter dyin', powerless to save her. Polly places the phone to her ear. She wants her final words to set her mother free. The doors begin to

22

close.

"Rosa," she whimpers. "Just like–" The doors snap shut. The phantom screams with rage. Never got to finish feedin'; Polly's blood decorates the platform. Her severed head bounces three times, then comes to rest beside a dustbin. Wild, empty eyes watch as the train pulls away with her body.

And what do you know? I guess a protagonist can be in two places after all.

The Sons of Satan

"That's quite the story you tell," Paul said with a smile, pouring the last of his drink down his throat. "Some kind of train phantom? Scary stuff. And right here in Kramusville, too! I almost believed every word you said–"

Fitz snorted into his ale.

"You've got to be kidding me."

"The tales are true, God damn it! Not one word fabricated! What business would I have o' spinnin' you lies, tell me that?"

"Besides free alcohol?" Fitz scoffed. "To scare the shit out of a couple of outsiders, perhaps? Giving the new boys a hard time is an old trick, Bastard."

"You watch your tongue!"

"Bastard's your name until you give me reason to call you otherwise."

The Bastard scraped his chair back and slammed his fists on the table as he stood. Fitz climbed to his feet, as did Paul, and in an attempt to keep the peace he placed a hand on both of them.

"Gentlemen, please! Let's keep things friendly, shall we?" Fitz glared but sat. The Bastard slowly turned to face Paul.

"Take your filthy fuckin' hand off me." Paul lowered his arm, and The Bastard straightened himself. "I don't intend on bein' *friendly* with a couple o' non-believers who turn their noses up to the facts."

"I don't turn my nose up to the facts at all; I turn my nose up to the fiction. As I said, I *almost* believed every word of your story. But those I had trouble believing concerned Miss Polly Whitmore's death." The Bastard narrowed his eyes; even Fitz was looking at Paul with a lack of apprehension.

"And why might that be?"

"Because I made a phone call to The Millerbank Hotel not much longer than one hour ago. And a receptionist by the name of Polly took the call."

Fitz smiled, then let out a short laugh.

"Peculiar."

"Didn't count on your audience being familiar with your characters, did you champ?" Fitz said with an air of sarcasm. The Bastard's stare grew fiercer yet.

"You think I give two fucks that you've heard Polly Whitmore's name before? I told you already; these tales I tell are real. Real events, real people. The fact you know o' Polly should have you crappin' in your tight whites, not darin' to question the authenticity o' her death."

"She's not dead, you sick fuck! Didn't you hear? She spoke to Paul on the phone!"

"Did she? Was she *really* talkin' to you, Paul? Did she acknowledge your words, exchange questions with answers?" Paul remained quiet for a moment.

"Not quite. There seemed to be a disturbance on the line. I heard her, but she couldn't hear me."

The Bastard sat back defiantly.

"That doesn't prove a thing! Paul still heard her voice!"

"What you heard was no doubt the voice o' Polly Whitmore's ghost. I've heard rumours that she still haunts The Millerbank, but I did not know she still took phone calls." He laughed darkly to himself. "Disturbance on the line indeed. And I bet *she* was the one complainin' about ghost calls, too."

Paul gulped. "Now that you mention it–"

"I cannot believe you are buying this bullshit! How do you suppose a fucking dead chick picks up a ringing telephone in a hotel? And then responds without a fucking head?"

"Polly got her head back. I delivered it to the morgue myself."

"Silly me. Of course you fucking did." Fitz stood up in a rage, and tugged his mobile phone from his jeans pocket. "Let's see what *Pretty Polly* has to say about that."

"You'll do well to get a signal in here, Mr. Muscle Man," Riley called from the bar. "We're somethin' o' a forgotten town." Sure enough, after pressing the phone to his ear, Fitz pulled it away and stared disapprovingly at the screen; then his face softened somewhat.

"Great. I've got a text from Rachel; must've come through earlier."

"Not checking in already, is she?" Paul laughed. "Put a ring on their finger and they'll do that to you."

"What? No, it's not that all. She just wanted me to call her when we got to the hotel, she's probably worried that I haven't contacted her yet." He turned back to face Riley. "Is there anywhere in this shit heap town that I might get a reception?"

"I seriously doubt that, Mr. Muscle Man. We're not ones for mobile devices such as that what you hold."

"I managed to get a call through back at the bridge–"

"If you think I'm going all the way back there now, you're mistaken."

"I gots me one o' them landline phones out the back. You start showin' a kindly ol' barman some manners an' he might let ya use it; for a small fee, o' course." His lips stretched to form a gummy smile. Fitz's face contorted, as though the mere thought of accepting a favour from Riley pained him, and through clenched teeth he spoke.

"May I use your phone? *Please*?" Riley continued to grin.

"Wasn't so hard now, was it Mr. Fitz?" He motioned with his head towards the curtain behind the bar. "You can have the first couple minutes on the house, but for every second thereafter, I'm gonna have to take me some o' your pretty coins."

"This shouldn't take too long," Fitz replied, as he slipped past the barman and beyond the curtain. Paul and Riley shared a brief glance, before the traveller pulled a stick of chewing gum from his pocket and pressed it between his teeth.

"So, what became of Ale–" Paul began, before turning to see that The Bastard was no longer sat beside him. He looked about the pub, searching for a sign of his whereabouts, but his eyes only came to rest once more upon Riley, who stood smiling with his ragged towel. Paul forced a smile in return, though his presence amidst an awkward silence unnerved him greatly. To relieve any tension, he stood and walked casually towards the bar. "*The Finger Inn*," he mused, once he'd decided what kind of conversation to strike up. "Quite a peculiar name you've got for your public house, Mr. Creeper. Any particular reasoning behind it?" The barman scowled awkwardly.

"'Cause I heard that 'fore you fuck your mother, you get her wet by stickin' the finger in," he spat. Paul frowned; the barman let out a hoarse laugh. "I do apologise, Mr. Paul. No one's truly sure o' how this place came to get its name, so we jus' tell that tiny joke we have here. Not much o' a legacy I know, but sometimes laughter is all we have. Pardon me for any offence."

"None taken," Paul replied earnestly. "I love telling jokes; the bluer, the better. My dad always used to say that the gift of laughter is a lot like anal sex. It's better to give than to receive; and all too soon, someone will start crying." Riley forced a wicked smile, and shook his head. "You got yourself a family, Mr. Creeper?"

The barman stopped cleaning; his smile faded slowly, and his gaze suddenly appeared forlorn.

"That I do not have, Mr. Paul," he replied softly. "Not any more. Used to have me three children; but they was taken from me, so they was." Paul gulped as a shiver ran down his spine; he hadn't intended on opening such a can of worms. He cleared his throat.

"I'm sorry to hear that."

"Little Nicholas was the liveliest o' the bunch. Always sayin' an' doin' things to get me into trouble, the little rascal. An' Thomas; well he wasn't much trouble at all, he jus' used to sit in front o' his television an' watch cartoons all day long. But my favourite–" Riley trailed off and allowed his head to drop. Paul stared sadly at him for a moment, and was about to extend a comforting arm, but the man composed himself. He let out a short, wheezy laugh, and looked straight ahead at Paul once more. "Gosh, that sounds jus' terrible, don't it? Havin' a favourite child? But my dearest darlin' Peyton; she was a sweetheart, so she was, Mr. Paul. She would do anythin' for her ol' man Riley."

Curiosity had gotten the better of Paul by now, and before he could prevent himself, he proceeded with his next question.

"Forgive me for asking, but what happened?"

"I had no woman in my life after Ladonna passed away. Seems some people thought I was unfit to take care o' the little ones on my own. So they stole 'em away from me."

"That's terrible," Paul said dolefully. A chair scraped behind him.

"That's only the half o' it," The Bastard interrupted. Paul spun round to see that he had returned to his table. "You think that's bad, wait until you hear the rest." Riley glared at him.

"I don't think Mr. Paul wants to be bored with stories 'bout his host. If he does, there's always the one 'bout yourself, Hanson. Maybe he'd like to hear that one instead."

"Why don't we let our guests be the judge o' that?" Just then, Fitz appeared from behind the curtain. Riley glanced at him, and then at the clock.

"Looks like you owe me some shinies, Mr. Fitz." He extended his hand; Fitz just stared at him vacantly, so Riley coughed and snapped his fingers, at which point Fitz pulled a note from his pocket and placed it in Riley's palm. Riley stared disapprovingly at the crumpled note, before removing a small amount of coins from his till and sliding them across the bar.

"Is that all the change I'm getting?" Fitz snapped in astonishment.

"Nothin' personal," Riley said, his trademark grin reappearing. "Jus' business, is all. Plus I noticed you're wearin' one o' my pencils behind your ear. Normally I don't command payment for such things; but *normally* people *ask*, they don't *take*." Fitz snorted in response and slid the coins back towards Riley.

"You may as well keep it."

"I don't take no charity; but if you wanna see them coins disappear into my till, you are more than welcome to make another purchase."

"I seriously doubt there's anything in this *fine establishment* that these coins could afford," Fitz replied with a short smile of his own.

"We gots a variety o' snacks–"

"I'm not hungry. Thank you."

"Well, that jus' leaves the jukebox." Riley nodded towards the machine in the corner. "But if you do decide to drown out the conversation, may I ask ya to be considerate an' not play anythin' by *Mia Bellezza*. Brings back too many bad memories." And he went back to cleaning his glass as the travellers moved away from the bar.

"I take it you got through to Rachel?" Paul asked as they walked back towards where The Bastard sat.

"Yeah."

"What did she say?"

"Not much. Amy started crawling earlier."

Fitz's response lacked any real emotion, Paul thought. "You'll regret missing moments like that, believe me," he replied. "You're going to be a family now."

Fitz didn't seem to acknowledge this remark, aside from rolling his eyes. He crossed to the jukebox and began to scan the list of tracks.

"What kind of jukebox is this?" he asked no one in particular. "I've never heard of any of these bands."

"That's 'cause they're all from Kramusville," The Bastard replied. "Riley didn't have any vinyl records to go in there, so when *BJs* opened, he started a collection." Paul and Fitz gazed at him, as though willing him to continue. The Bastard just nodded at Fitz. "Go ahead, pick a song. They're crap mainly, but there's a few I reckon would be right up your alleyway."

"Oh yeah? And what exactly is *my alleyway*? Strike you as the rocking type, do I?"

"Well you sure as hell ain't into no hip hop! And the way you bully that muscle man body o' yours around, I'm guessin' you ain't into easy listenin' either. You like your music loud and heavy. And Four Eyes here? Don't yank my chain and tell me you're not into soul."

"I'm partial to the old rhythm and blues," Paul replied. "What about yourself?"

"I'm easy. As long as it's done right, I'm a fan."

Fitz inserted his money and pressed a couple of buttons. The machine whirred into life as the arm removed the disc from the carousel and placed it on the turntable; the stylus swivelled as the disc began to spin, before the sound of hard rock blasted out of the surrounding speakers. The Bastard leaned back in his chair.

"The Sons o' Satan," he declared confidently, his eyes pinched shut now as he lost himself in the music. A brilliant bass line combined well with an epic guitar riff as cymbals thrashed in the background. A male vocalist demonstrated great range; verses of deep and meaningful lyrics sung with such authority, and stitched together by an anthemic chorus. Paul and Fitz found themselves nodding along in time to the beat, picturing this band up on stage, performing with a presence that suggested they were more than just a small time outfit from a town that nobody had really heard of.

This is you, this is me, this is unity!
This is everything that you could ever want to be!
Such a lie, but who am I to burn the effigy?
Such a shame, that the flame was never verbatim!
Twist my words while I write another synonym!
For the hatred that you feel for her and him.

You seem so proud when you forsake our bed,
You scream so loud that you could wake the dead...

Suddenly, an ear piercing shriek burst through the air, as the track came to a shuddering halt, snapping the travellers from their daydream. The Bastard peeled his eyes open slowly and stared at them.

"You hear that scream?"

"Hard not to!" Paul replied. "I didn't just hear it, I felt it!"

"Curdles your fuckin' blood, doesn't it? Gets me every time. You know why?" The Bastard sat up straight. "That's the sound o' a young man dyin'."

"How'd you mean? As in the narrative of the song?"

"No! I mean that scream was the last noise to ever escape the mouth o' Logan Short."

"What, did he die shortly after or something?"

"He died durin' the recordin' o' that song." The travellers exchanged a sceptical look.

"And what kind of sick fuck would leave a dead man's dying scream in the final mix of a song?" Fitz asked.

"The same kind o' sick fuck that killed him!" The Bastard replied, slamming his fist on the table. "Still, you can't blame him for wantin' his revenge." The travellers edged closer.

"Go on," said Paul, urging him to continue, but The Bastard remained quiet.

"You know the rules, Four Eyes." He tapped the empty glass before him. "Buy The Bastard a brandy, and he might just tell you a tale about this town."

"For someone reluctant to tell us their first tale, you're sure eager to tell us a second," Fitz said wryly.

"And for someone who refused to believe the death o' Pretty Polly, you're sure eager to hear o' Vannigan's grudge. But just like every other story, it's gonna come at a price. You wanna hear the facts, you're gonna have to foot the bill."

Paul flinched as he turned to face the bar. "Creeper!" he called. "Same again. And pour yourself one, too." Riley just smiled.

"Credit where credit is due, Mr. Paul," he replied, and he began to fill glasses to the brim. "You're learnin' the rules fast."

Tale 2

V annigan's *G rudge*

1

There used to be a recordin' studio on Renegade Street. A proper shitty underground place called BJ's; the kinda place that only bands you've never heard o' would go near. Big Joe Patterson ran the joint when it first opened. Daddy's lottery win paid for all the equipment, o' course. Joe was in a band called The Cock Suckers for all I care; biggest pile o' shit around, with Big Joe on bass guitar. It's sayin' somethin' that he was the best player in the band, 'cause he was fuckin' awful! The singer sounded like a cat havin' a watermelon shoved up its ass, the drummer couldn't beat for shit, and I doubt the guitarist had ever seen a six string in his life. The whole thing was a shambles, the songs were terrible, and the only record they ever made was a five track self-titled EP I had the misfortune o' listenin' to back in the '80s. They had plans way above their station, thought they were gonna be the next big thing; Big Joe said they'd be Kramusville's answer to The Stones. But when no one turned up to their big debut show, and every copy o' their record was returned with cries for refunds, they called it a day.

Thank fuck.

Anyways, Joe decided to rent out his recordin' studio; fairly cheap at first, but once interest had generated, he was chargin' nearly one hundred notes per hour. And people would go there, record a couple o' tracks, send out dozens o' copies, get rejected, and end up tryna make a pretty penny outside Carmel's Record Store 'til he chased 'em down the street with a double-barrel that is, and then the likes o' Ragin' Ramona and Twisted Fuck Knuckle were never heard o' again, with any luck.

But then, outta nowhere, came this one band that blew everyone away.

Logan Short and Albert Vannigan had been friends since their schooldays, and were practically joined at the hip. Never saw one without the other. Everythin' they ever did, they did together, like they were fuckin' carbon copies or somethin'; except Albert was short and chubby with shoulder length black hair, while Logan was tall, thin and conventionally attractive, with a tangle o' blonde curls and a lip piercin'. Anyways, they both dropped outta school at the same time, took shitty jobs in a warehouse and spent most o' their evenin's down at The Pelican, this bar where all the cool kids would hang out to smoke pot and watch live music. I believe that's where they met Donny Langford and Simon 'Clipper' Harris; another couple o' losers who just so happened to possess some serious musical talent. Donny on the electric guitar, and Clipper on the bass.

Why did they call him Clipper?

I don't fuckin' know, maybe his dear mother Mavis cut hair for a livin', stop with the fuckin' questions already!

Anyways, they got talkin' and Vannigan lets on that he can play the shit outta the drums, while Shorty has always fancied himself as a lead singer. And after a few neat rums, and plenty o' puffs on the funny shit, they decide to form a band.

3

They got their shit together and started practicin' a few weeks later in The Langford's garage, with the door up to get the attention o' passers-by, and I remember walkin' past durin' one o' their rehearsals; even then I was impressed at what they'd managed to put together. I mean, the lyrics weren't great; Vannigan's creative writin' talent was stretched to stringin' weak rhymes together, and every other word was a curse.

Fuck the prick who holds the bat,
I'll cut him first and that'll be that.

You get the idea?

And Vannigan didn't even have a full drum kit at the time, so they did well to make do with what they did have. But they were full o' energy, jumpin' around with next to no clothes on, drinkin' and smokin' and workin' up a sweat. Called 'emselves Flo & Co. at first, after this local girl they'd all claimed to have had sex with. But then the crazy cat lady at number 32 caught sight o' their naked rock playin' antics and said they were the spawn o' the devil himself.

So they changed their name to The Sons o' Satan, and wrote a song especially for crazy cat woman. Whether she was aware that she was the pussy with the pussies they were crazy to tap, I'll never know.

Then suddenly they start practicin' these really catchy numbers, I mean catchier than before; crazy ass guitar riffs; deep and broodin' bass lines; Vannigan invested in a proper drum kit and was playin' these incredible solos; and Shorty was showin' a lot more range, hittin' notes so low you damn near shit yourself, and notes so high you had to question if the guy had himself a cock and balls at all. And the lyrics became dark and beautiful, proper heartfelt shit with meanin'. I think Donny's brother wrote most o' them; quiet boy never seen without a notepad. He had so much teenage angst since their dad walked out, and he was harbourin' it like it was goin' outta fashion.

Summers bleed until they end,
Winter is my only friend.
Cold embrace me, we unite as one.
The love we've got could freeze the sun.

Quite possibly my favourite track; they first played that one at the open mic night at The Pelican. Had 'emselves a fair few fans by the end o' that gig, too; about the only act that got any kinda applause for their efforts. Well, they kept doin' shows, and by the seventh, eighth, ninth gig they had the whole damn crowd bangin' their heads, and singin' along to every word. Kramusville is known for secrets kept, but somethin' like The Sons o' Satan was never gonna remain secret for too long. Suddenly, there were kids comin' from other towns to hear the band everyone was talkin' about. Word o' mouth, old school shit; none o' this Facetube crap. Next thing you know, there's rumour o' a big label signin' 'em up, and so the band get 'emselves down to BJ's to record a self-titled EP.

And naturally, that was when disaster struck.

4

Daddy never helped with homework,
Daddy never played our games!
Daddy never really knew us,
Doubt he ever knew our names!
Daddy dearest was always working,
Down in Hell amongst the flames!
Daddy killed us just like the others.
But love for Daddy still remains!

We four we rise as one!

We are the sons of Satan!
The Devil never knew what we'd become!
We die young, we are the sons of Satan!

You like that shit? That was somethin' o' a signature track. Used to save that number 'til last when they played their shows; y'know, heighten the anticipation, then go out with a bang. I remember the last show they performed together; they played that song and every fucker in the crowd was singin' along and bouncin' into each other like a God damn lunatic, it was quite somethin', I tell you. The guys would stay around for a drink or six with their fans, they were good like that. And then they'd stagger off into the night, usually to crash at Donny's; but on this particular night, Vannigan gets talkin' to this redhead with a chest on her the likes o' which I'd never seen. The other guys head off, but he stays behind to sweet talk his way into her panties. O' course, there's no way I'd know exactly what he said to that chick, but whatever compliments he threw her way, it worked, 'cause he left that bar not thirty minutes later with this stunner on his arm. And seconds after, he was lyin' flat on his face at the roadside.

Vannigan falls foul o' a speedin' car; the thing just comes flyin' outta nowhere and throws his body like a fuckin' rag doll through the air. He lands so hard on the concrete, all twisted and shit, we're sure he's dead. The driver o' the car musta been off his face on somethin'; he goes for another half mile then slams into a wall, comes flyin' through the windscreen and crumples in a heap. The redhead was unrecognisable after they'd pulled her body from beneath the wreckage; poor girl went straight under the wheels and got scraped down the street, left this horrid bloody smear behind. She stopped screamin' as the car passed the tattoo parlour, so I'm guessin' she died before she was crushed between metal and brick.

The doctors can't do anythin' to save the redhead or the driver, but Vannigan's still got a pulse somehow, so they work through the night to save the guy's life; more specifically, to save the guy's arms, they're a fuckin' mess. Let's just say they managed to reshape 'em; but either way, the poor kid's not playin' the drums again.

5

A couple o' months later he's allowed to leave his hospital bed, heads straight to Donny's garage to meet up with the others; they're all mad excited to see him back on his feet, but none too pleased to see his arms all in plaster, and his fingers not quite pointin' in the right directions. Soon as he heads home to grab some shut eye, the others start conspirin'. See, they figured he couldn't play anymore, what with both his arms broker than a dog-faced prostitute. But Vannigan would turn up to practice every evenin', watch the others, try to join in, all the while Dr. de Nero's tellin' him he'll be lucky to ever hold a drumstick again. The rest o' the band knew they were gonna need a new drummer; they also knew that Vannigan would never allow it.

Funny that his body should be found a week later; police said he'd been the victim o' a random attack. With three bullet holes in his chest? I don't fuckin' think so! Shorty, Donny and Clipper pulled the trigger once each, I don't care what anybody says. They couldn't decide who should kill him, so they all did it. They even hacked off both his legs, so that he couldn't 'hit the foot pedals in hell.' Only scum would do that to contradict the lyrics the man had written. I'm surprised they didn't leave a knife hangin' out the poor fuck's back. Next day, Seann Glover fills the vacant position in the band. The Sons o' Satan were back in business.

6

They buried Vannigan a few days later over at the cemetery on Cesare Street. I remember the service well. Me and Emily went, as did most o' the town. Stood beneath umbrellas in silence as they carried his casket, set it down beside the gravestone. Albert Vannigan, aged 23, gone but not forgotten. Poor kid's mother couldn't bring herself to speak, and what with his dad barely playin' a part in his upbringin', he didn't exactly have a speech prepared either. So the only one to say a few words before they lowered him into the ground was Logan Short. And I gave him the dirty stare throughout his little fuckin' sob story.

"Albert was like a brother to me. I can't believe he's gone, taken from us so young. We did everything together. He was about to hit the big time; it was his dream. Without him, the band has lost its meaning. We were close to pulling the plug altogether, but we knew Albert wouldn't have wanted that. He truly was, *is*, a great person, and he wouldn't have wanted us to give up on our dreams too. The fact that we will realise that dream without Albert is very unfortunate, and saddens us greatly; but we will take to the stage now to preserve his memory, his legend. And whenever we bring The Sons of Satan to a new audience, Albert will live on through that. I love you, man."

And he tosses a single flower onto the casket lid as they bury him six feet beneath us, sheds tears with Donny and Clipper, and for a brief moment I sense a great deal o' remorse from those murderous cocksuckers. But they're back in the recordin' studio before the guy's corpse has even started to rot.

And that beautiful line they sang about wakin' the dead was about to become a nasty reality for The Sons o' fuckin' Satan.

7

They spend the best part o' a week recordin' material for their album. I guess they're not entirely comfortable committin' songs to vinyl that Vannigan had some involvement with, so they lay down only new tracks. But somethin' is eatin' away at Logan. Maybe he genuinely does feel remorse killin' off his best friend like that; so one night, after a long day in the studio, he pitches an idea to the rest o' the team.

"*The Ballad of Machete Mike* seems out of place on the album, don't you think?" he says, takin' a swig o' mineral water. "It feels too conceptual compared to the other tracks. Maybe we should save it for the next record." The others trade weary glances, they've been playin' all God damn day, they just wanna crawl beneath their duvets and lay fresh stains on their pillows, so they all nod in agreement, but Logan isn't done yet. "Let's replace it with *Wake The Dead*." The room was pretty silent anyways, but it somehow gets quieter. Clipper leans on his guitar.

"Do you think that's such a good idea? I mean, Albert wrote that song."

"Yeah," Donny pitches in. "Maybe it's for the best if we leave our older songs alone."

"But it's a perfect fit! We start with *Lifetime of Summer Afternoons*, and end with *Wake The Dead*; we transcend into darkness over the course of the album, and with the theme of relationships apparent throughout, it makes so much sense to include the song." They all look to Seann at this point, I guess they're wonderin' if he minds drummin' a dead man's part on record. I mean, he'd played all their old stuff a couple o' times in rehearsal while they were writin' new songs, but they'd always said this was just to integrate him into the band better, get a feel for their sound. Seann just shrugs his shoulders. Big Joe pokes his head round the door.

"You haven't got too much time left, guys," he says. "You might want to finish up another day."

"We just need another few minutes," Logan replies. Joe disappears. "I'm not sure we can afford to spend another day in here. Let's just lay this track down in one hit; we've been playing it for so long, I doubt it'll need much work." Donny and Clipper pick up their guitars, Seann takes up his seat behind the drums. Logan grabs the mic, pinches his eyes shut tight, gets in the zone. "1, 2, 3, GO!"

8

You ever had a sleep where you didn't dream?

You can't recall any pictures movin' before your closed eyes, no little movies playin' in your head, nor any sounds to accompany 'em; Hell, you can't even remember only darkness, or the air that has escaped your nostrils as your chest softly rose and fell, and it's like the last eight hours o' your life you may as well have not been breathin' at all. I guess that's the closest I can make you feel to Vannigan in that coffin, what with him bein' dead and shit.

Now imagine that you are dead, too; and you know you're dead, 'cause the last thing you saw was your best friend aimin' a loaded gun at your beatin' heart, while the rest o' the band stand behind him waitin' to curl their own fingers round that trigger to end your life. You don't anticipate a thing to follow, except an endless rest that you're not gonna remember a thing about, 'cause you're fuckin' dead, right? Stay with me here.

What if you came to life again?

What if somethin' woke you from your death, like an alarm clock wakes you from your sleep? It's like somebody paused your life the second you lay your head on the pillow, or the moment the bullet pierced your heart; you become a shell, whether it's for eight hours beneath a duvet, or for a fortnight bein' moved from a crime scene to a mortuary to a hole in the fuckin' ground, and then that alarm sounds and your eyes snap open again. To the sound o' Beethoven's seventh symphony from your bedside cabinet.

To the sound o' your killers playin' a song you poured your soul into.

Vannigan exhales that final breath he took; his brain goes into overload, commandin' every inch o' his body to do somethin', *anythin'*, all at once, and he collides with the insides o' his new home. For a split second he panics, questions why there is suddenly only darkness when before there had been light, and Logan, and the gun...

It all becomes apparent; he knows he is dead, he knows because he is in a casket, beneath six feet o' soil, and yet his lungs aren't cryin' out for oxygen. He knows his life ended at the hands o' his best friends, his band mates, and he knows he can feel the vibrations and hear the sounds o' a song he composed the night his first love broke his heart. All the sadness he once associated with that track consumes him once again, but it quickly subsides, replaced by a violent rage, sees red through the black, smashes his head against wood, fists against wood, feet against...

"My legs." Vannigan reaches down, feels his legs with his fingers, but can't feel his fingers with his legs, if you see what I mean? Fumbles around for a moment and grimaces when he discovers that they're not attached to him at the hip. And then he only gets angrier, assumes a greater strength somehow, begins to forge holes in the casket lid, spits dirt from his teeth as it seeps through, before the holes become so big that he is showered in a mass o' black; and just like when he was dead, he cannot move once more. And it seems as though he's gonna lie that way forever, nothin' happens for a good couple o' minutes, but just when it's lookin' like the worst comeback in history, the shortest lived revival you've certainly ever heard about, the surface begins to shiver and out screams this defiant fist. Vannigan pulls himself free from his restin' place and basks for a brief second in the cold o' the night air, bathes in moonlight, embraces everythin' he never knew he missed in death, and then he hears the faint finale o' his song and he tells himself that revenge will only be sweet; soften the blow o' never realisin' the dreams he once had. The Sons o' Satan made a big mistake in becomin' murderers, but they made an even greater error o' judgement when they buried Albert.

They shouldn't have buried him with his sticks.

I've seen some crazy shit in my time; seen a checkout girl pleasure herself durin' openin' hours, even watched a burnin' buildin' crumble to the ground, and seen a man step from the ruins with a song on his lips and not a care in the God damn world. But if you'd happened to pass the cemetery that night, you'd have seen a dead guy, severed from the waist down, with broken arms pullin' his way across the dirt usin' two thin wooden skin beaters.

And boys; shit don't get much crazier than that.

9

Logan screams the final note; Seann improvises a little drum solo to end on as the sound o' the guitars fade to silence, smashes the cymbals once more for good measure.

"That was perfect!" Clipper cries. "I don't think we've ever played it that well!" Maybe he's tellin' the truth, maybe he's bullshittin' 'cause he's sick and tired o' those four walls, but Donny and Seann nod in agreement either way. But Logan isn't entirely happy with it. Reckons he stuffed up a line on the second chorus.

"It sounded fine to me," Donny tells him, but Logan's his own biggest critic, and somethin' o' a perfectionist. Wants to record that part o' the song again; but see, the others aren't so willin', and what with Big Joe makin' exaggerated gestures with his watch behind the glass, they start movin' towards the door.

"Come on, Logan," Seann says. "It was a great take. Stop being so fucking hard on yourself. You've hardly slept while we've been making this record. Get some rest, for fuck's sake." And Logan can't help but acknowledge this fact; he smiles weakly at the guys.

"You three can head on home if you want. I'm just going to add some backing vocals, and then I'm done with this place." Donny, Clipper and Seann head out into the hallway, while Logan signals to a tired Joe for two more minutes.

"Do you really think he's just adding backing vocals?" Donny asks out in the hallway. Seann shakes his head.

"No chance. This album has taken over the man's life. I'll bet he's adjusting every tiny thing to make it sound like the greatest record ever to grace the ear of man. He's fucking deluded! We might be big in Kramusville, and in these neighbouring towns, but we're not world beaters just yet! What we've recorded these past few weeks is the shit; I say we leave it as it is, put it out there, get much needed exposure, and if this record company decide to put their money where their mouth is, that's when we iron out the flaws and give them something better."

"That's what Albert would've said," Clipper says quietly.

"Yeah? Well, maybe you killed the wrong guy." The lights go out in the corridor. They instinctively stop walkin'. The lights flash back on, black out again, and then slowly flicker into life once more. The three o' them are starin' at each other in bewilderment, wonderin' what the fuck is goin' on. And then *Wake The Dead* begins playin' softly; they're not sure how, it's supposed to be in a soundproofed booth with Logan, but it's out there in the corridor with them too, and it's startin' to get louder and louder. And then Donny sees it, his eyes bulge, they're damn near outta his head they're so wide, but before the others can catch sight o' the same thing, the bulbs overhead become a blindin' white, obscurin' the figure ahead, and they shield their eyes.

"What the fuck is happening?" Seann yells.

"What did you see?" Clipper asks, strainin' his sight to see through the brightness, panic settin' firm in his voice.

"It's Albert. It's fucking Albert."

And Clipper really starts freakin' out when he hears that.

"Shut your fucking mouths!" Seann spits. "The guy's dead! You watched them put him under the ground, you thick fucks!"

"He's here," Donny starts to repeat. "He's here. He's here."

"You guys are fucking retarded, the lot of you! I'm out of this fucking band, you hear? Let your dead fucking friend back in for all I care!" And he begins to storm down the corridor as the lights get even brighter, then suddenly they explode, showerin' them all with glass as they're left in the dark yet again. Seann stops; and a pair o' drum sticks rattle against the marble surface underfoot.

They start runnin', the sound o' hurried footsteps barely audible over screams and the ever increasin' volume o' their song; they try to escape but they only collide blindly with each other. Clipper takes a tumble, smashes his face on the floor. Donny begins chokin', and Seann swings aimless fists at the noises he's makin'; he can hear Donny thrashin' about, knockin' shit off the walls, then he slumps into a pool o' his own spit. Clipper lets out a cry as somethin' rips into his flesh, pulls out his innards, and Seann tries to get the Hell out when he hears bones crunchin', meat snappin' and slurpin', but he slips on a trail o' red and falls heavy through a pane o' glass. He tries to pull himself up but can only cut his hands to shreds; then somethin' grabs his hair, thrusts his head onto a jagged piece that ends his life in an instant.

Big Joe has heard the commotion, he's out in the corridor too, and he has to grab a flashlight when he flicks the light switch to no avail. And he starts to shit in his pants when he sees the dead bodies; Donny's throat has been squeezed so tight that his larynx is juttin' out like a serrated rock on a cliff edge, and his face is a pale veiny mess; Clipper's stomach has been opened like a fuckin' book, and all the juicy shit therein has been left strewn across the floor, like a trail right outta Brothers Grimm classic; and Seann, slumped over a window pane, his eyes wide and lifeless, the shard o' glass speared right through his temple. Big Joe spins round in terror, and the beam from his flashlight falls on another dead body. But this one is barin' his teeth at him, eyes pulsin' with venom, and before Joe can even utter Vannigan's name in confusion, his heart is ripped from his chest; and just like that, he is dead too.

10

I guess Logan had been too wrapped up in his vocal work inside the booth to notice that Big Joe had gone; he's lost in the sound o' his own voice, singin' as the track plays into his earpiece. But then it goes deathly silent, and he looks up to where Joe was moments before, only to stare into the eyes o' the best friend he never thought he'd see again. There's a tiny bit o' elation in there, I'm sure, outweighed by shock, certainly overpowered by fear. His mouth begins to tremor, but before he can utter a single word, Vannigan breaks the silence himself by playin' the track at full volume into Logan's ear; he drops to his knees in shock, tears the headset off and throws it to the ground.

"Albert, I–" He tries to talk once more, but Vannigan shuts him up by rattlin' his two bloody drumsticks together for Logan to see.

And then he holds up Big Joe's stagnant heart to really incite the fear.

Logan doesn't manage to keep his dinner down, and he screams like a little bitch when the drummer slams a claret handprint onto the glass. Vannigan just stares at him. Logan's shittin' in his pants under the watchful eye o' the writer slash composer slash best fuckin' friend who happens to not be alive anymore; and then Vannigan turns his attention to the dials in front o' him.

"W-what are you going to do?" The song starts to play into the booth.

Logan wipes his face roughly with the palms o' his hands and climbs to his feet, as Vannigan disappears from sight. His eyes are dartin' everywhere, he figures the dead can just emerge from thin air at will; but then the door surges open and there's Vannigan pullin' himself into the booth, and Logan backs up against the wall. The man's a fuckin' wreck. For someone tryin' to make a livin' outta usin' his voice, Logan can't get his excuse out for shit; it just sorta tumbles out like one big word as tears stream down his face, and he's got sick and spit sprayin' from his mouth and everythin'.

"Albert-I-can-splain-wassen-me-ah-swear-jus-lemme-splain-I-wassen-finkin-it-wassen-me-ah-swear-jus-lemme-talk-oh-jesus-christ-jus-gimme-a-chance-I'll-may-kit-better-I-swear." Vannigan just pulls himself closer as the track continues to play, his face now shakin' with rage; and if things weren't fucked up enough already, he starts to growl along to the song at the top o' his voice.

Once a friend, 'til the end, is now the enemy!
Only pain can break the chain of this fidelity!
Saw you fly, soaring high coz baby now you're free!

"Albert please–"

Hope it's worth, time on Earth, filled with deep regret!
When you rediscover love we shared the day we met!
I'm positive that I won't forgive and won't forget.

"Albert–"

You seem so proud when you forsake our bed,
You scream so loud that you could wake the dead...

Vannigan leaps through the air, slams his right fist forward and spears a drumstick right through Logan's eye, and Logan lets out that brain meltin' shriek you boys are now familiar with. He falls to the ground, and Vannigan just stabs away at him until his heart stops pumpin' blood through his veins. Exhausted, he collapses on top o' him; and you know, for a brief moment, it's just like the old days.

Logan Short and Albert Vannigan. Never saw one without the other. Like carbon fuckin' copies; except Albert was short and chubby with shoulder length black hair, while Logan was tall, thin and dead.

With a tangle o' blonde curls and a lip piercin'.

The Paimacozine Drag

Fitz took a sip of his drink, held it in his mouth for a moment, then swallowed with a frown. "Are the lights going to fail in every tale you tell us?"

The Bastard eyed him curiously. "The fuck is that supposed to mean?"

"The lights on the train flickered, the lights in the corridor flickered; we're not stupid, Bastard. We're very aware of the suspense you're trying to create, but there must be a different cliché device up your sleeve."

"Rollin' power shortages are commonplace in Kramusville when the weather is bad in the evenin's," Riley called from the bar. "It's why I burn me some candles instead; ain't no frightful storm gonna put me in the dark. Most o' us establishments are festooned with candlelight round here, Mr. Fitz."

"And the supermarket down the street?"

"The Eight-Til-Late?"

"Their lights seemed fine to me; and they definitely weren't candles I saw lit up inside. Weather's pretty fierce this evening, wouldn't you agree? Do you see where I'm going with this?"

The Bastard snorted as he threw the last of his brandy past his gums.

"You think I'm feedin' you more lies 'cause the supermarket lights didn't flicker in the instance you walked past?"

"No," Fitz replied earnestly. "I think you're *feeding us more lies* because every other fucking light flickers in the instance of someone dying. Never mind the improbability of someone's head *actually* being severed by closing train doors, or the recently deceased *actually* coming back to life."

"Are you callin' me a liar?"

"I'm just questioning your abilities as a storyteller, that's all. You're trying to sell us these tales as fact, and yet you're expecting us to believe the impossible. Now, I'm willing to suspend disbelief when it comes to dialogue; there's no way of you knowing what conversations took place behind closed doors. I'm even ready to accept character backstories; maybe you know for sure about Polly's childhood trauma, maybe you don't, but adding depth to your protagonist is never a bad thing. But I will not sit here and tell you that I believe for one second that Albert Vannigan rose from the dead to kill his band mates. I get what you're driving towards; *the scare*. The big chill down my spine.

"But you're too explicit, too definite. Logan's death would've had a far greater impact if you'd only alluded to Vannigan's involvement. Maybe the dirt around his grave appeared scattered in a peculiar fashion, maybe his drumsticks turned up at The Langford's garage, or maybe Logan's body was found severed from the waist down, clutching a copy of *Wake The Dead*. No one can claim to know for certain what happened that night, but the signs are all indicative of the same thing. And the not knowing for sure, the supernatural becoming an almost rational explanation for the unknown; that's where the fear lies, Bastard."

"Well ain't you the loquacious one!" Riley laughed from the bar, but The Bastard's eyes only grew narrower.

"Who the fuck are you?" he asked. "Am I in the company o' the finest horror writer without realisin' it?"

Fitz sat back in his chair and smiled.

"Let's just say I'm a keen reader."

"I'm listenin'."

Paul let out a short laugh, and playfully hit Fitz with the back of his hand.

"We work for a publishing company a fair few miles from here," Paul said. "Maybe you've heard of us? Amdion Press."

"I told you already, I don't concern myself with fiction."

"We work with biographical materials, too. In fact, there's not a lot we won't work with. We're pretty versatile when it comes to genre, but very selective when it comes to print. Only the finest works get to grace the same page as the Amdion logo. I'm chief editor of our crime department; currently working on the latest *Fate Knox* instalment. And my good friend Fitz here is part of a team that deal with horror submissions for our quarterly magazine. Every writer receives a personal response; I guess that explains his constructive criticism."

"I think there's a little more to it than that." The Bastard leaned closer to his guests, glanced between the two for a while, before slowly nodding his head. "Yeah, I can see it now. The wounded look in your eyes, Mr. Fitz."

"What look?"

"Wrote himself some horror fiction growin' up in an idyllic little home by the sea. Mommy and Daddy used to say he was the next big thing, but then Daddy washes up on the beach, and Mommy; well, she just wants to get away from it all, sells up and moves her only son to the city. Promises that every little thing is gonna be alright, but the kids at the local school don't take to the new boy much, do they? Label him a freak for spendin' all his free time in made-up worlds with the characters he's created, steal his lunch money, give him a bog-wash two or three times. Would explain why Mr. Fitz here started workin' out. Gave the bullies a taste o' their own medicine, became somethin' o' an anti-hero, revered by the unpopular kids.

"And this new Fitz gave up on his dreams o' becomin' what Daddy had told the locals his precious offspring would become. Spends the next years o' his life workin' part-time at the gym, resentin' most o' his lifestyle choices to date, but then our four-eyed friend here comes along with a job for him at the publishin' house, so he takes it to rekindle the flame. And all it's served so far is to let him sit and judge manuscript after manuscript, tellin' himself that he could do better; but see, he doesn't know if he can do it any more, does he? And Mr. Fitz reflects that negativity on the storytellers around him. Have I got it about right?"

"You couldn't be further from the truth if you tried."

"So what exactly have you been puttin' down in that notebook o' yours, the recipe for mamma Fitz's famous cookies? Don't think I haven't noticed you scribblin' away durin' my tales; no doubt reducin' me to ridicule while plannin' your own spin on events. I've never considered myself a muse before. Should I keep my eyes peeled for the tales o' Pretty *Penny* and Albert *Flannigan*? Or is that notebook gonna sit upon your shelf, unused, just like all the others?" Fitz laughed as The Bastard leaned in closer. "Answer me this; just how many submissions have you personally accepted since your employment commenced? I'd wager only a handful, and that those lucky few got the all-important Mr. Fitz green light 'cause his boss was on his back. Face it, hotshot; I've got you sussed. Tell me I'm wrong. Here's your chance to spin me a tale for a change."

"You want me to tell you a story? I've got one for you; it's called The Bastard Drunk."

"Funny that."

"Do you want the abridged version? Hanson drops out of college before the final exams, fails to land a job, marries his counsellor, drinks away his benefits, becomes a widower. Or do you want to know all about the tear in the contraception the night a married businessman had a drunken one night stand with a teenage reveller; a girl who decided she wanted to keep the baby, and accepted a large cash sum to keep her mouth shut and move away to a town that next to no one had heard of. She christened the bastard child Hanson, raised him the only way she knew how; with a stiff drink in one hand, and a stiff dick in the other, alternating between the taste of the two, telling her wide-eyed baby child that this was his daddy, only for a host of different gentleman to come and go, quite literally."

"Gettin' a little personal now, doncha think?"

"It would explain why all your characters so far have had terrible fathers." There was a deathly silence as everyone waited for The Bastard's response; even Riley stopped cleaning his glasses as Paul gulped quietly, while Fitz just grinned defiantly, certain he had the upper hand. Finally, their host spoke once more.

"The relationship I shared with my father was just fine, not that it's any concern o' yours. The events that I recount, I did not write; and my *characters*, as you like to refer to them, are their own personalities. But what about you, Fitz? What about *your* characters? Are they separate entities, or are they subconscious reflections o' the author himself? That wounded look in your eye, it goes deeper, I see that now. That body you watched 'em pull from the water - the man your mother married, the man who raised you as his own, the man you called 'Dad' until that fateful day - well, he wasn't your father at all now, was he? You've never known your biological old man; you've never known him, but you know that you hate him for his absence, and you hate 'Dad' for dyin'. You hate all fathers. Especially yourself. You said you'd be a better father than any other; but one unplanned pregnancy later, you've realised you're just the same."

"I am nothing like my father."

"And why's that? 'Cause you're always there? Like hell you are! How much o' Amy's childhood have you already missed out on? She started crawlin' earlier, right?"

Fitz stood and grabbed The Bastard by the coat.

"Say one more fucking word and I'll take your head clean off your shoulders, I swear!"

"That's not you talkin', Fitz. That's your father." For a moment, it looked as though Fitz was about to smash his right fist into The Bastard's face, but at the last second he slammed his knuckles into the table instead. He headed towards the men's toilets, barging the door open with such force that it shook on its hinges.

"How did you know about his daughter?" Paul stammered quietly.

The Bastard straightened himself up.

"Sometimes we hear things that we're not supposed to," he replied. "You o' all people should know that, Paul."

"Excuse me?" And then suddenly, music began to play from the surrounding speakers. Paul recognized it instantly as Patsy Cline, but it certainly wasn't her voice singing along.

I fall to pieces, each time I see you again.

A voice so sweet, so beautiful, so near.

I fall to pieces, how can I be just your friend?

"Who's this singing?" And Paul found himself shouting over the increasing volume of noise. Other sounds started to fade into his ear; scattered applause, the occasional cheer, bar stools scraping, whispered conversation. Confused, he began searching around for an explanation, but found none.

"There's no one singin', Paul," The Bastard replied, but his response was barely audible.

You want me to act like we've never kissed.

"What's going on?"

You want me to forget, pretend we've never met.

"What's happening to me?"

And I've tried and I've tried, but I haven't yet.

Paul was pressing his ears firm to the sides of his head, shaking violently to silence the voices, but to no avail.

You walk by and I fall to pieces.

Fitz, alerted by his friend's yelling, appeared in the toilet doorway, just in time to see Paul tip backwards in his chair and land violently on the floor.

"What the fuck did you do to him?" he cried, rushing over to Paul to find his eyes fluttering.

"My head."

"What the fuck happened? I swear to God if he's hurt–"

"I'm fine."

"–I will fucking open you, do you hear me?"

"Honestly, Fitz, there's no need."

"I will cut you the fuck open!"

"Fitz!" Paul began to sit up, and with Fitz's help he found himself once again on his chair at the table. "I told you, I'm fine. I just need some headache tablets, that's all."

"Do you have any aspirin?" Fitz asked Riley, but the barman shook his head slowly.

"'Fraid not. I'm not one to keep tablets; not for medicinal purposes, anyways."

"What happened?"

"I heard voices again. A woman singing this time. *I Fall To Pieces.*" The Bastard and Riley shared a glance. "My head was agony. Are you sure you don't have any aspirin?"

"Yes, I'm sure!" Riley snapped. "I ain't one o' them consumer fetishists, buyin' things jus' 'cause the movin' pictures tell me to! If my body is clever enough to start hurtin', it's surely clever enough to correct itself, dagnabbit!"

The Bastard placed a thin stick on the table.

"Suck on this," he said. "It kinda works like a cigarette, but it's loaded with *paimacozine*. If that doesn't fix your head, nothin' will." The travellers read the words inscribed on the side of the object; *May Cause Awesomeness.*

"I don't get it," Paul replied earnestly.

"Jargon; seduces the target audience, y'see. Part o' the *Kool Kidz* range. Products aimed at impressionable youngsters; makes 'em believe they'll be popular if they're smokin' fake cigarettes, or drinkin' fake alcohol, or wearin' fake cologne. There was initial uproar, o' course; but then they discovered that the manufacturers were loadin' their goods with *paimacozine*, and the crap really hit the fan. See, it's a drug that targets the nervous system. Works real fast, too. A small dose won't do you any harm; in fact, it'll do you the world o' good. Relieves the pain, provides temporary release just like any other analgesic. But too much, too often, and you'll get addicted to the stuff. Course, the boys and girls were goin' crazy for *Kool Kidz* items. And they were gettin' hooked on the *paimacozine*. And that's how Gina got 'em. Go ahead, take a drag; if that don't see you right, then that ain't President Grant starin' back at you from a fifty dollar bill." Paul flinched, and after a moment's deliberation he hesitantly lifted the stick, Fitz watching him all the while with a look of concern. He slowly pressed it between his lips, and took a deep inhalation.

"How do you feel?" Fitz asked, as Paul replaced the stick onto the table, and exhaled gradually.

"Strange. I feel great. I mean really good."

"Told you."

"I'm having me some of that." Fitz picked up the stick and took a long puff himself. "Madness."

"As always," The Bastard said. "Déjà fuckin' vu."

"What do you mean by that?"

"I've observed it a hundred times over; monkey see, monkey do. If Four Eyes here hadn't taken a dose, you wouldn't have either, and with good reason. You're not in any pain. Nonetheless, you see how fast it acts, and you're intrigued; so regardless o' your fit state, you have to try it for yourself, but answer me this: what good is that *paimacozine* doin' in *your* system?"

"Besides making me feel even better?"

"Precisely. It does *nothin'*, except provide that ephemeral high. Ain't that how every addiction starts? Who can deny 'emselves euphoria when it's in the bottle that they squeeze by the neck, or in a neat line on the coffee table, and lyin' naked on the bedspread? Tell yourself that once was enough, and you tell yourself a lie. Look me in the eye and say you don't wanna suck on that stick again already."

Fitz slid the cigarette across the table towards The Bastard.

"My will's a little stronger than that," he said with a wicked smile. "But I guess I'd be fooling no one if I said I didn't want to take one for the road."

Riley let out a strange sound; a cross between a snort and a laugh. "Well look'e here! Mr. Muscle Man wants to be one o' the *Kool Kidz* again! I s'pose you'll be askin' for a brand new pair o' sneakers next, an' a top o' the range mountain bike. Heavens to Betsy! Darn advertisin' ain't ever done nothin' but brainwash them kids. That television box turns 'em into zombies. Ain't that the truth, Hanson?"

The Bastard shook his empty glass. "Fill these up, Riley," he replied. "This one's on me."

Tale 3

C_{lean} $U_{p\ on}$ A_{isle} G_{ore}

1

A kid wakes up with a pain rippin' through his skull. He is old enough not to scream, but young enough to want Mommy to kiss it better. One problem.

Mommy's dead.

And Daddy's workin' the night shift at Benny's Bowlerama. No shit. The kid's got two choices. Lay back down and try to get some sleep. Or ask Daddy's new wife, Lucille, for some headache tablets. Lucille's gonna be none too happy if she has to miss a few frames o' her late night omnibus; either way, the kid's gotta suffer.

He waits for a moment or two, watches the second hand on his bedside clock tiptoe slowly past the others, before decidin' he can take it no more. He kicks off the bed sheets, slides off the mattress, slips into his favourite band t-shirt.

Which band?

What do you mean, which fuckin' band? How am I supposed to know, I wasn't there, you sick fuck! And I don't know which brand name he had stitched into his pyjama bottoms either, so stop askin' questions.

But what I do know, at least I reckon so anyways, is that the kid's headache only got worse as he creaked his way down the staircase, and closer to the sounds comin' from the television. *The Cobbled Avenue*, episode one million and six; Raymond confesses his love for Joanna yet again, blah blah blah, just cut to the sex scene already. But stepmommy Lucille is so engrossed in the crap, she doesn't even know the kid's in the room until he's standin' right next to her and says her name.

"Jesus Christ! You little rat bastard, you nearly scared me to death!" She breaths heavily, tries to calm, tries to keep one eye on the kid and the other on the television screen. "I thought I told you to go to bed two hours ago, why are you still up?"

"I've got a headache."

"So take an aspirin."

"It's hurting real bad."

"So take two, then!"

"I can't reach the medicine cupboard."

Lucille roars angrily, thuds barefoot into the kitchen, opens the cupboard above the sink and rummages through a basket o' medication.

"We don't have any." The kid looks at her. "Don't look at me like that, it's not my fault we don't have any!" The kid continues to look at her *like that*. "What do you want me to do? Drive to the store and buy you some?" The kid nods. "Forget about it! You tell me at a quarter to midnight that you need aspirin, and you expect me to jump through hoops? Well guess what? I've got a headache, too. It's you, you little rat! Now get up to bed!"

A kid makes enough noise complainin' about the pain, and eventually his stepmommy shuts off the television and grabs the car keys from the fruit bowl.

2

Do you know how hard it is to find a store open at that time o' night?

The answer?

Very. And I'll bet you every bottle behind the bar that Lucille said the same exact words to the kid as they sped down the street like a greyhound outta trap six. All the while he writhed in the back seat like an atomic bomb had gone off inside his head.

"You best not be faking, you little punk! If this is just some snot nosed prank to get off school tomorrow, you're for it! You understand? I'm missing my soap operas for this! So you better be dying, you hear me!"

The car skids round a corner, nearly hits a rabbit or somethin'.

Do you like rabbits?

Cats.

Well, the car skids round a corner and nearly hits a cat, then.

A big, black, bastard o' a pussy cat.

Its name?

Are you shittin' me, wise guy?

It doesn't matter what the cat's name is, 'cause it ran off and has no further involvement in this story. Not now, not ever! In fact, thirty seconds later, it was probably gettin' some shut eye up a tree, just as Lucille was turnin' into an empty car park outside the Eight-Til-Late on Morgan Avenue.

"Wait in the car!"

"But it's dark outside."

"So? I'll be two minutes!"

"I'm scared."

"Boo-hoo, you little brat!" She climbs outta the car and slams the door, screws her face up when she sees that the kid has done the same. "Stop playing games and get in the car! I don't have time for fooling around!" The kid just stands there starin' at her like some kinda invalid. Lucille barks like a dog. "Fine! Come with me, then. But if you so much as look at the magazine stand, I'll give you something to cry about! Come on!"

The cold o' the night air stings their faces as they walk, and a breeze pushes 'em gently towards the slidin' o' automatic doors.

3

You know how you can never find what you're lookin' for in a store when time is o' the essence, no matter how many times you shopped there before? Well, Lucille had been doin' her weekly shop at the Eight-Til-Late for as long as she could remember, and picked up aspirin from aisle seven so many times she could probably tell you the layout o' the whole damn store if she wanted to. But she is flustered as fuck, rushin' around to get back in time for the last minutes o' the show. She walks straight down aisle one, glances around like a loon for tablets in the groceries, all the while cursin' like a mad woman.

"Fucking pain in my ass, needing tablets this time of night, who am I, the fucking pill fairy? Shitty little punk, takes after his no good God damn father, he should be the fucking one taking care of the kid, I'm not his fucking mother."

She shoots the kid a look, wonders whether or not he's heard; and I guess a part o' her wanted him to, a vindictive part that blamed the kid for anythin' and everythin' that had gone wrong with her life recently. But another part wanted him to have been blissfully unaware o' her little comments, if anythin' to prevent another argument at home with the kid's father, though I guess deep down she had grown kinda fond o' the little bastard, she was just too stubborn to admit it, even to herself. They bypass the next few aisles, but Lucille can't resist headin' down the hot drinks aisle to grab herself a jar o' cheap caffeine.

Always the way, right?

You go into a store, knowin' exactly the one thing you need to buy, yet you wind up with a full basket by the time you reach the tills, pay for things you neither need nor particularly want for that matter. I went shoppin' for groceries with a girlfriend once; came out with another girl's number and a bruise the size o' Satan on my right cheek. And a bottle or two o' brandy, o' course.

I suppose you wanna know her name as well, right?

Well it wasn't my Emily, that's for sure; she was worth three or four the Vals and Sals o' this earth, cross my heart and hope to die. And she was worth a damn sight more than Lucille, too; some might reckon she deserved to die, the way she dragged the kid by his hand towards the checkouts like he was nothin' but a damn doll, his tiny little shoulder threatenin' to pop right outta its socket. Others would argue that she deserved to live; and if she'd known what that little punk was only minutes away from inflictin' on her, she woulda surely broken both his arms, and got outta that store with more than just a container o' coffee beans, but with her heart still beatin' too.

4

Terry Atkins watches the last pin fall down, then hits the light on lane six.

"Yo, boss man," one o' the bowlers shouts. "One more game."

"Sorry, but we're closed," Terry replies in an oh-so-calm manner, prepares to recite the script he'd been taught on day one. "I'm going to have to ask you to leave." More often than not, the punters would acknowledge this fact; they'd quietly leave the premises, and then Terry could lock up. Occasionally, they'd argue, and so Terry would return to the script he'd memorised, keep a polite and professional demeanour, threaten to hit the red button beneath his desk; they'd leave the premises a little louder than they otherwise could have, and then Terry could lock up. And then there was the rare instance when they'd do more than just argue, as they happened to on this night.

"I don't think you heard me. My friends and I would like to play another game, hit the lights." There were four o' them in total; two chicks who thought they were way hotter than they were, and two pricks who had obviously heightened that self-obsessed opinion in their attempts to get laid. And the way the guys were constantly checkin' their phones, I'd say their attempts weren't exactly above board, if you see what I mean?

"Let's get outta here, Chris," one guy says to the other.

"No chance! Polly just called, cancelled our plans for tomorrow night. You know what that means? I haven't got to rush anyone out of my apartment. I'm going ball deep in that blonde tonight, and then the bitch can make me breakfast in the morning, lunch in the afternoon, and if she cooks as good as I fuck, I'll make sure she gets dessert after dinner."

"Well, you can take the brunette, too. Maybe she can cut your food up with her thong."

"What is wrong with you?"

"Nothin'. I'm gonna have a night in with Sal tonight, that's all."

"Look at Mr. Moral over here. Need I remind you that she's not your wife?"

"Need I remind you that we're closed?" Terry interrupts. "If you could kindly take your dispute outside–"

"What the fuck did you just say?"

"If you could kindly take your disp–"

If you're evidently an asshole, there's only one thing worse than being told what to do; it's havin' the same command repeated, word for word, when you ask 'em what they said in a rhetorical way. Chris was evidently an asshole. If ever there'd been a doubt in my mind, it was erased when he started throwin' bowlin' balls at this innocent employee.

Terry Atkins was somethin' o' a gentle man. Had to be around six foot tall, weighed 175 pounds, and was fairly quiet. Never had much hair; not even sure I can recall him havin' eyebrows. If he did, they were blonde, and thin, and barely visible above his beady brown eyes. Always clean shaven, always polite and professional, always looked a shadow o' a man. I guess the passin' o' his wife only softened the poor guy, and quite how he ended up with a loud-mouthed skank like Lucille for a second spouse is beyond me. I reckon he panicked at the idea o' raisin' the kid on his own, and put a ring on the finger o' the next vagina that presented itself to him. Either way, Terry Atkins was somethin' o' a gentle man.

At least, we thought he was.

Musta been an alter ego bubblin' just beneath the surface. A kinda repressed entity, that hadn't been allowed to surface when the bullies made fun o' his eyebrows, when the kid was born and looked nothin' like him, when Teresa died in the house fire. But see, Terry had read the script forwards and backwards, countless times, and he could read it to you word for word from memory. And there was nothin' in the script that told how to politely and professionally respond to someone throwin' a bowlin' ball at your face while screamin' obscenities.

So he proceeded to pull out a gun.

5

Assholes like Chris usually only understand one language; *asshole*. It is a dialect that only assholes can adopt and perfect, one that causes 'em to reject all other languages, and so respond only in asshole. But apparently, they also understand the silent tongue o' the firearm. The girls ran screamin' from the buildin'; guess they got the message loud and clear, too. But Chris interacted a little longer; he nodded, as though answerin' any questions the gun had, as he sidled quietly towards the exit. His friend apologised unreservedly, but Terry said about as much as the gun did, and before long he was left alone in the bowlin' alley, sobbin' soundlessly to himself, the gun still poised in his hand, and he too held a brief conversation, though he was shakin' his head. He threw the gun down, and rifled through the pockets o' the jacket placed on the back o' his chair, pulled out a cigarette. Puts it in his mouth, tries to light it, takes a puff, spits it to the ground.

Recognizes the taste.

The taste o' *paimacozine*.

He looks at the side o' the cigarette. Sure enough, there's that *Kool Kidz* logo. Terry ponders just how it had come to rest in his pocket. 'Cause he specifically remembers stoppin' the kid's pocket money so he couldn't try to buy those products himself. He'd even stopped believin' the kid when he said he was unwell, certain he was addicted to the *paimacozine*, lookin' for his next fix. Terry's phone vibrated. A message from Lucille.

Kid sez his not feelin gd, needs asprin, where can I buy this tym of nyt

Terry had his suspicions that Lucille had been givin' in to the kid for the sake o' an easy life for some time now. This wasn't the first *Kool Kidz* cigarette he'd mistaken for his own in recent memory. There he was, tryna be the assertive father, like Teresa had always wanted him to be; and there was Lucille, underminin' him, tryna be the cool stepmom, no doubt for her own selfish reasons. What did she care if the kid had a drug addiction? If he was up in his room gettin' high on analgesia, he wasn't interferin' in her life. She probably woulda bought him another dog too, despite her allergies, if it meant some peace and quiet at the expense o' a few sneezes. Terry didn't hesitate in tappin' out his reply.

8-til-Late.

6

Lucille stands by the checkouts; aspirin in one hand, coffee jar in the other, and she's achin' to get back home to catch the rest o' her show, but all the tills are empty. Reckon Gina, the girl who works the graveyard shifts, had gone for an early piss break.

"Fucking great." Lucille juggles her shoppin' into one palm, grabs her phone from her jeans pocket, rings Terry.

"Hello? Yeah, we're in there now, but no fucker's around to serve me. Am I sure the kid is sick? What do you mean am I sure, the little shit swore to me on his life that he was! What did you want me to do, let him suffer? Let Daddy come home and find his precious shit of a son dead on his mattress? Well, if you're so sure, Dr. Prick, why don't you ask the kid himself–" Lucille turns round and the kid is gone. "Where'd you go, you little punk?" she screams. "I told you, no funny business, didn't I tell you that?" She starts stormin' her way back through the store, eyes down every aisle tryna find him, but no such luck. "No I haven't lost him! Oh you want to question my parenting ability now?

Because you're such a great father! Yeah, well we'll see about that when you get home tonight, won't we?" Lucille ends the call as finally she spots the kid, standin' halfway down the aisle o' fizzy pop and energy drinks. His eyes are drawn to one shelf in particular, just stood there starin' like it's abstract art or somethin'. "What did I say, you freak? No fucking around! Get your scrawny little a–"

"Shhhhh." Lucille stops talkin'. The kid slowly turns to face her. "They're coming."

7

A loud screech tears through the store, before a female voice erupts from the speakers.

"Clean up on aisle seven."

The sound o' marchin' footsteps from all directions, slow, rhythmic, almost hypnotic if you will. Lucille looks up to see a group o' five, maybe six, kids walkin' down the aisle, turns and sees another six comin' from the other way. She stands upright, wonders what the fuck is happenin', and then she notices somethin' else about these kids besides their flawless marchin' synchronicity. They've all got plain, bright white eyes, as though they didn't have an iris between 'em. And they are armed to the teeth with weapons.

Most have got knives or lead pipes, one cute little girl no older than eight years old is cradlin' a hammer like it's a newly born brat. A scruffy little tyke over the back obviously didn't get the memo, he's picked up a train set and he's havin' the time o' his life without killin' anybody. But the rest o' them? They go to work on Lucille in next to no time at all. Momentarily they stop and stand and stare at her, she's confused, but then it's like all these little switches flick on inside their heads, and they begin to carry out their dirty work strategically; Gina not seen, but pullin' the strings like an invisible chess player. A blade slices through Lucille's Achilles tendon, and she screams murder as she drops to her knee, and then this freckly kid takes out her other leg from the knee down with a swing o' his axe, and there's a sea o' blood which Lucille can only slap at wildly as she tries to crawl to freedom. And then the girl with the hammer starts slammin' away at her elbows, breaks 'em both without too much trouble, and the taller boy with the lead pipe gets tired o' her screamin' so he breaks her jaw and shoves his weapon down her throat, punctures her vocal cords, and Lucille can only make this hoarse whisper as her mouth fills with that metallic taste. She manages to claw weakly at the kid's trouser legs, pleads silently with him to help, and he does in a way I guess, in that he puts her outta her misery with a firm foot to the temple, and as she starts to go stiff on her back, he starts slicin' away at her neck like she's a wheel o' cheese or somethin'.

Bring me the head, Gina commands telepathically. And the kid picks it up and walks over to till six swingin' Lucille's head like it's a fuckin' cabbage, gives it to Gina. She's this ugly hag o' a woman, and she's only about to get uglier as she lifts one leg up to rest upon the till. She's not wearin' any panties, and she's so wet I swear she's got juice drippin' like her pussy's a leaky faucet. She takes Lucille's head in both hands, runs fingers through her hair and makes that dead woman go down on her; straight up, she's thrustin' her hips into the face and cryin' with delight, body shakes and everythin', but the sickest part I guess is the way she controls the kid, makes him watch, while the rest o' her merry gang o' murderous minors hack what's left o' the kid's stepmom into teensy pieces and start baggin' her up like she's the fuckin' weekly grocery shop.

8

Terry brings his car to a halt outside the Eight-Til-Late; he's *too* late. He can already see the kids comin' to the doors with their bags full, watches silently as they march in time and load 'em into the boot o' Lucille's car.

And then a broad smile spreads across his face when he sees his son, marchin' at the rear, carryin' a lone bag, and for a split second Terry is certain that their eyes meet, but even through the darkness he knows that Gina has him now. He is torn between grief and glee; he had never wanted it to come to this, but in that moment he decided that perhaps it was for the best.

Terry held his mobile phone in his hand. He had killed Lucille, he knew it. She had betrayed his trust, and deserved to die, right?

He is not your son, Gina said. He picked up his gun, and once more he held a silent conversation; except this time he nodded in agreement. Terry placed the gun into his open mouth. It was as though Gina had command over him as well.

9

Terry held the matches in his hand. He had killed Teresa, he knew it. She had betrayed his trust, and deserved to die, right?

"He is not your son," Gina said, placin' an arm around her brother's gentle frame. "You shouldn't burden yourself with raising another man's child alone." Then she slowly turned to face him; her plain, bright white eyes burnin' fiercely. "Let me take him."

"I'll never let you take him," Terry replied. "The day my son becomes a part of your sick cult, will be the day my brain decorates the furniture!"

And, true to his word, Terry pulled the trigger.

The Broken Pact

Fitz couldn't keep the smile from his face as he finished the last of his ale, and a short laugh escaped his lips as he placed the glass once more on the table.

"You are too fucking predictable, Bastard. I highlight the fact that all your father figures have been bad guys, and the next one out of your mouth is Jesus Christ himself."

The Bastard stared at him, dumbfounded.

"I don't know what Bible you grew up with, kid, but I don't remember the son o' God ever wieldin' a firearm."

"Maybe not; but I bet Terry was a complete piece of shit before you conjured up a sob story to make him something of a likeable underdog, tortured by the ghosts of days gone by but redeemed by a kindly sacrifice. But guess what? I don't buy it."

"There's a fuckin' surprise."

"The story was too rushed! And there's a whole host of gaps throughout. You give us next to nothing to work with, and I certainly don't care enough about any of the characters for the ending to have any real impact."

The Bastard threw the remaining drops of his drink past his lips and sighed.

"You'll make up your fuckin' mind, Mr. Publishin' House. If your 'constructive criticism' told me anythin', it's that you wanted me to spare you the borin' part; not that I consider any aspects o' my retellin's to be borin'. But no one really wants the wordy scientific introduction now, do they? They just want the horror to kick in, so they can tell the rest o' the book club if it made 'em crap in their panties or not. I gave you boys somethin' o' an abridged version; fast forwarded past Dr. Domizia's discovery o' *paimacozine*, skipped the *Kool Kidz Kompany*'s inception in the late 90s, even bypassed Gina's first supernatural experience back when she was a little girl herself."

At this point, Paul cleared his throat and joined the discussion.

"That's something I was meaning to ask," he said. "How is Gina able to control the kids with her mind? Don't you owe us that explanation?"

"Does anyone really ever know how or why certain people are blessed or burdened by the art o' telepathy? I could hazard a guess, but I wouldn't want you boys to *suspend your disbelief* any more than you're willin' to."

"Of course not," Fitz replied. "And that's why you'd introduce the totally plausible notion of a group of zombies killing late night shoppers. I mean, are you fucking serious? People disappear on a late night shopping trip, and no one thinks to investigate? Maybe try to shut down Gina's little operation?" The Bastard exchanged a glance with Riley, before slowly turning back to face the travellers.

"Let's just say the authorities were a little preoccupied."

"Preoccupied or not, an army of the undead sounds like a pretty big deal to me. What about the rest of the town? Seems everyone has a gun, but not one person fancies their chances as a vigilante."

"Or have the common sense to stay away from the Eight-Til-Late," Paul added. "I'm sorry, but if people were aware of what Gina was doing to those poor children, and not had the urge to try and prevent it, the very least they could've done was stay away."

"'Cause you haven't got a curious bone in your body?"

"Excuse me?"

"Someone tells you not to say The Boogeyman's name five times in the mirror, else he arrives in a puff o' smoke and tears your heart out; so what are you gonna do the next time you're combin' your hair or brushin' your teeth? You're gonna convince yourself that no such entity exists, 'cause everyone's a sceptic 'til they see it with their own eyes. Curiosity gets you sayin' his name once, twice, maybe even three times before a gust o' wind or a creakin' floorboard makes the hairs on your neck stand to attention; and then fear really sets in as you whisper his name the penultimate time, makes you wanna stop this little game, get out while you still can, escape with your life before it's too late. But curiosity will inevitably triumph. Maybe not on that first occasion, but certainly the next time you find the courage to summon The Boogeyman. And the clean up on aisle seven worked in the same damn way. Once the rumours got round, o' course everyone laughed it off at first. But the next time they found 'emselves approachin' the Eight-Til-Late with a little one in the back? 'You know what, let's do this tomorrow night.' Or they'd keep on drivin', do their shoppin' in the next town for a change. "I heard about some great deals in the store a few miles from here." That's the fear, you see. But then the empty cupboards from those postponed shoppin' trips, or the empty rainy day jars from those extended car journeys, will see the curiosity prevail. Before long, you find yourself with a full trolley at checkout four, laughin' to yourself about how stupid you've been lately. You turn to share a smile with your daughter, or rustle the hair o' your son, only to discover that they're no longer stood alongside you. Go ahead, call their name, they won't hear you; they only respond to Gina now. You check down every aisle, and for once in your life you'd probably hope to find 'em lyin' bleedin' amongst glass or holdin' hands with a creepy lookin' old stranger; as long as they're not starin' wild eyed halfway down aisle seven. But o' course they are. Your heart doesn't miss a beat when you see 'em, nor does it beat so fast that it threatens to leap from your mouth; The Boogeyman already holds it in the jaws o' his vice." Fitz smiled.

"A heart in one hand, and a cell phone in the other, right?" The Bastard raised an eyebrow in confusion. "Who do you think would have The Boogeyman among their list of contacts? Pretty Polly? Maybe Chris or Terry? Even Lucille, perhaps?"

"Care to enlighten us with what you're drivin' at, Fitz?"

"For a town not too familiar with mobile devices, a lot of your characters sure seem to have one; that's something of a discrepancy, wouldn't you agree?"

Riley let out a short, high pitched laugh from the bar.

"Dear me, Mr. Fitz!" he cried. "You really do concern yourself with the funniest o' things! Polly Whitmore gets attacked by a phantom, an' you ponder the strength o' train doors. Albert Vannigan rises from his grave to kill, an' you question the shortage o' power. Gina Atkins forms a cult o' killer kids, an' you consider only the method o' communication. All these stories o' death an' devastation, an' you're still worryin' 'bout them pennies I charged you for a phone call!"

"I don't think Fitz was worrying about the fee to use your landline, Mr. Creeper," Paul said hastily, before Fitz could respond in a less than friendly manner. "He was merely doubting the legitimacy of mobile phones in Hanson's stories."

"And why might that be?" The Bastard asked.

"Because when he tried to call–"

"It doesn't matter," Fitz interrupted. Paul shot his friend a look of confusion.

"What do you mean? Of course it matters. When Fitz tried to call Rachel–"

"Will you let it go already?"

"What is wrong with you? Don't you want to know why–"

"Not really, no."

"But–"

"No buts! I know what you're going to say, and it doesn't fucking matter. So can we just forget about it?"

"No we cannot," The Bastard snapped. "If you boys have got somethin' to say about one o' my tales, you best give it to me quick; or else Mr. Fitz here won't be the only pissed off person at the table, and I will have to *take* those words from you with force. Do you understand?" The travellers exchanged a glance; Fitz shook his head, but Paul was adamant.

"I'm not sure what your problem is," he said, "but I want an explanation." He turned to face The Bastard. "If these tales are as true as you claim, how could Polly call her mother–"

"Paul, please just leave it."

"–or Terry text his wife–"

"Paul, I'm asking you nicely."

"–when a signal is so hard to come by that Fitz couldn't contact his fiancée?"

"Paul!" Fitz spoke his friend's name so fiercely that even The Bastard was stunned. "She's not my fucking fiancée, ok? Never was, never will be." An ugly silence fell upon the pub. Paul looked at Fitz for a few seconds, as though initially unsure of what he had said, but then he suddenly understood, and his voice cracked slightly as he replied.

"Excuse me?"

"She never said yes. She doesn't see a future for us together, as a family."

"But the text message … You said Rachel wanted you to call her when we got to the hotel."

"To make sure I hadn't done anything stupid! Am I so fucking unhinged, that she'd believe I'd throw myself under a train because she doesn't want to be my wife? Do you know what she said when she picked up the phone? That she'd almost started crying, thinking that I had killed myself because of her, and wondering what she'd tell Amy when she's old enough to ask about her dad. Do you know what she said next? That she consoled herself with the idea that she could be as close to a nice normal family as possible with her next boyfriend, without me turning up out of the blue every now and again and messing with poor Amy's head. She said they're better off without me, Paul. She said I'm never there, anyway; and I may as well be dead." He paused for a second as he lowered his head, almost ashamed to show his face. "Amy started crawling earlier. She'll send me letters and photographs, on the condition that I stay away from them both."

The silence this time was even uglier. Paul glanced away from his friend to survey the expressions of their company. The Bastard genuinely looked mournful, as did Riley when Paul motioned for him to top up their glasses. The sound of ale slurping from the pump would be the only one to fill the air for a short while, aside from the heavy contemplative breathing of the travellers as they both stared down at their shoes, lost in thought.

"I am so sorry, Fitz," Paul suddenly said gently, as Riley placed their drinks on the table and waited to accept his money.

"You have nothing to be sorry for," Fitz replied. "This is all my fault. Despite everything I grew up telling myself, I still turned into my own fucking dad. And the worst part? That piece of shit read me like a fucking book!" He looked up from the floor to motion towards The Bastard, but once again he had disappeared.

"If it's any consolation to ya, that S.O.B. is far from a model citizen himself," Riley piped up as he returned to the table to set down a small amount of change before Paul. "Some o' the things you said 'bout him earlier weren't exactly a million miles from the truth, either. He claims to have had a good relationship with his dad, but fact is, Daddy died 'fore he was even born. Maybe Hanson sees that as a positive thing. If there never was a relationship, then nothin' negative coulda happened to make it a bad one. I, for one, disagree; the bond between parent an' child is struck as soon as your little swimmer fertilises that sweet woman's egg. If anythin' should happen to sour that bond 'fore the child is born - I dunno, let's say Daddy gets shot by his mistress' husband - you don't start afresh when the doctor introduces you into the world. You never look your child in the eye; an' that, my friend, is a bad relationship."

Riley took a long thoughtful sip of his own mineral water. "Maybe bad fathers like yourself jus' connect, Mr. Fitz." Fitz slowly turned to face Riley, and not for the first time that evening it seemed as though he was about to smash his fist into the barman's face. He did clench his hand tightly into a ball, but to Paul's astonishment, this was only to collect the change from the table; then he stood, only to walk over to the jukebox. He shoved the coins through the slot and pressed a couple of buttons. Once again, the machine whirred into life, shortly to be replaced by the slow gentle sound of a piano. Fitz turned to face the table, where Riley was slowly lowering his drink from his mouth. "You dirty boy."

"Care to sing along for us, Mr. Creeper?"

Somebody, somewhere, loves me.
Somebody, somewhere, cares...

Riley's face was contorted with rage. He slammed his glass down on the table.

"I oughta rip your face right off!" Before Paul had a chance to react, Riley charged forward. For a man so frail in appearance, he moved with alarming pace, and had The Bastard not suddenly appeared to place a strong arm across him, it seemed as though Riley would've indeed torn Fitz's head clean from his shoulders.

"Not like this, Riley!" The Bastard roared, and the barman stopped struggling to straighten himself up.

"What on earth has gotten into you?" Paul asked.

Somebody whispers God into the night,
Hoping he'll hear their prayers…

"I asked you boys real nice, not to play anythin' by Mia Bellezza. You dirty boy; you dirty, dirty boy." And with that, Riley stormed back to his bar and beyond the curtain. The Bastard sat down.

"That was a rotten trick, Fitz."

"He provoked me. I got him back the only way I knew how."

"You'd better hope to God he's calmed down when he comes back; don't let his appearance fool you, that man is capable o' killin'." Fitz snorted, but Paul shot him a disapproving look as The Bastard picked up his brandy and drank it in one. "Another brandy, another tale. The one I've got about Saltzmeister is gonna turn your brains to crap."

"Is that so?"

"Do ducks have bills?" Paul flinched as he stole a glance at his watch. There was a little under three hours remaining until the train was due to arrive at St. Arthur's Walk station.

"Wait," he said quickly, before The Bastard could begin. "Have you never picked up a book before, Hanson? Don't you think it's a little late to be introducing us to new characters? Maybe you should tell us a story about a character we've already been introduced to." The Bastard looked at him perplexed, but quickly understood what Paul meant when his eyes darted towards the curtain behind the bar. The Bastard just laughed.

"I'm serious! I want to know about that psychopath's messed up past!"

"Seems you've got a pair o' balls after all. You saw what the man wanted to do to your friend after hearin' a song; imagine what he'd wanna do to you if he heard those words escape your mouth."

"What's stopping you, Bastard?" Fitz called. "When this night began, you were willing to let us dictate the nature of the tale. What's changed?"

"There are some stories that you just don't tell outta courtesy."

"Like the one about your dad, for example? I mean, who'd want everyone to know about their old man eating lead while pumping some of his own behind his wife's back?" The Bastard leapt to his feet again.

"Who the fuck told you that?"

"Who'd you think, Einstein? It's not like Paul or I have known you all these years. That no good fuck told us a little story about you; I say fuck courteousness, and tell us a little story about him."

The Bastard eased back into his chair, contemplation decorating his face.

"We had a deal. The darkest days o' our lives would remain in the shadows for as long as we both shall live; sheltered by our entities, so that not even the sun itself could expose 'em, only sheddin' light on what the others could see. He broke a pact–"

"So break it back."

Someday, someday,
The moon will show us one day.
Inside we yearn, for that fires burn,
Someday, someday...

The Bastard snatched up Fitz's glass and took a great gulp of ale.

"I'll do more than break it," he said darkly. "I'll fuckin' destroy it."

Tale 4

Mr. Creeper (part I)

1

Somebody, somewhere, needs me,
Somebody, somewhere, true...

A distant scratchin' is enough to wake her; at first, she chooses to ignore it, closes her eyes, tries to sleep once more. But the sound not only occurs again, it persists, and so she sits up, dries drool from her lip and slips her feet into slippers to investigate. Her hair is wetted to the side o' her head; she wipes crust from her face as she treads wearily from the room, carefully towards the staircase. Breathes heavily, has to lean, has to medicate, finds the tablets in her cardigan pocket, raises a shaky hand to her open mouth, dry lips purse and she takes it in like a pro. Lets a minute or two pass before she shuffles her way cautiously back to bed, though not before a quick stop at the bathroom to splash water on her face and stare mournfully at her reflection in the mirror. It had been this way for as long as she could recall; had to be a mouse, she assures herself, the scratchin' always stopped when she reached the staircase, had to be a mouse, she wasn't crazy, not now, not ever. Not yet anyway; mouse, had to be a mouse, and then the front gate swings open outside. She glances outta the window and watches him walk the path towards the house, his briefcase swingin' in one hand, keys janglin' in the other with a jaunty tune escapin' from his child friendly smile.

Mr. Riley Creeper.

Let's reacquaint ourselves, shall we?

Don't you think for one second that I'm gonna leave out Mr. Creeper's big introduction. I don't care that the man's been stood right behind you all night; I'm the one tellin' the tales, remember? And I always give the characters a brief descriptive passage; helps the listener visualise. You don't like that, you know what you can do. And anyways, Riley wasn't such a fuck ugly goof back when this tale was set. I mean, he was tall, thin, and he had a mouth full o' teeth for himself, not to mention two eyes that he had control o'. And he always made sure his hair was slicked back; the ladies liked that look apparently.

And he wasn't just a bartender in a beaten up inn, neither; he used to run a chain o' shops down by the bridge. See, that little strip o' shops used to make quite a pretty penny back in the day; especially with the rumours flyin' around that most o' the place was haunted, Kramusville became somethin' o' a tourist attraction over the years. People would take the train in, take photos outside BJs, shop at the Eight-Til-Late, and they'd love to cross that damn bridge, long before any reputation it garnered. They used to call it the battered bridge, play a game called *death crossin'*, see if they could make it to the other side and back in one piece. The bridge was a little more stable than it is now, but they always got a thrill outta it rockin' sideways above the train tracks. And Mr. Creeper back there, well he saw an opportunity, opened up a gift shop, used to have kids draggin' their parents in there to buy all kinds o' mementos. Printed t-shirts, sticks o' rock shaped like bridge slats, even fuckin' paperweights made to look like Pretty Polly's head. Sick shit, but they loved it, they thought it was all urban legends and that these toys were morbidly cute. They didn't even think the *Kool Kidz* stuff Riley had on sale was real either, just like replica memorabilia from your favourite fuckin' movie. Used to wind me the fuck up; course, Riley didn't care. Those ignorant little pricks were linin' his pockets. Guess it'd been a good day at the office, 'cause he was particularly cheerful as he entered the house, placed his briefcase silently by the fireplace, and climbed the stairs with a cry for his beloved.

"How're you feelin' today?" he asks, plantin' a firm kiss on her moist forehead. She just scowls at first. "Is the medication helpin' at all?" One nod for yes. "An' the new mattress? Are you sleepin' any better?" No response. "Ladonna? Are you sleepin' any better?"

"I've been praying that someday is in sight, and hoping he'll hear me too."

"What was that?"

"I heard it again. With voices this time." Riley laughs softly.

"Mother, that's jus' a song. I keep tellin' you, there's nobody else here. Is that why you're all sweaty? Did you get outta bed?"

"I heard it again. I had to be sure."

"You've gotta stop this. The doctor said you'll only make things worse." Ladonna lies there, cries silently, and Riley looks upon her with great sorrow. "I love you." He presses his lips to hers, kisses her like no son ought to kiss his mother. She just lies there and takes it. Riley heads to the doorway. "I'm makin' a pasta sauce for dinner. Try an' get some rest." And he closes the door so that she cannot see tears formin' in his own eyes; tears o' sadness that quickly turn to anger.

He storms down the stairs and unlocks the second o' three doors. A young boy turns away from his television screen to look at him.

"How many times have I warned you 'bout the volume, li'l boy?" Riley hisses. He tears towards the child with his arm raised, and the poor kid shields his face with one hand and with the other points a quiverin' finger to the corner. Riley looks to where the kid is pointin', and sees another boy holdin' the control between his teeth. "Nicholas? How did you get outta your room?" Riley hurries over to him now, grabs him roughly by the collar o' his shirt and carries him to the first room, opens the door and throws him inside. He starts whimperin', but Riley quickly shows him the needles and Nicholas soon shuts up. "One more word from you tonight, an' our little friends here will make sure you don't see nightfall. Understand? Now sit down on your chair, or you ain't gettin' fed." Riley watches him sit, then closes the door, locks it, checks, double checks, heads back to the second room, the kid is peekin' through his fingertips. "Dinner will be in an hour, Thomas. You can watch your television 'til then, but if the volume creeps up again I'll fetch Mr. Hammond."

Thomas shakes his head fiercely at the thought o' the hand puppet.

Riley closes the door, locks it, checks. And then he breathes deeply. And then a smile spreads once more across his face as he approaches the third door, opens it, and slowly descends the concrete steps.

3

"It's a peculiar feelin'; wouldn't you agree, Peyton?"

The girl sat with her spine pressed firmly against the wall; the coldness o' the brick against her back was in stark contrast to Riley's hot breath, which steamed up the thick rimmed glasses perched on her freckled face. Peyton turned her head away, only to be reprimanded once more.

"What did I tell you?" Riley said softly, though there was a tinge o' ire in his voice. Peyton sniffed sadly, but Riley wasn't satisfied with that as a response. "Peyton? What, did I, tell you?" His hand moved sharply, and the girl held back a scream before replyin' with haste.

"You-said-that-if-I-moved-or-made-any-loud-noises-you'd-break-one-of-my-dolls."

"That's right." Riley smiled, and he kissed the girl's forehead. "I don't wanna break your toys, Peyton, but I mus' apply these guidelines; you understand that, don't you?" Peyton nodded nervously. Riley brushed her cheek with the back o' his hand. "I love you." Her scalp was itchin' terribly, but she refrained from scratchin', for fear o' watchin' one o' her beloved doll's bein' destroyed. They were her only friends. Without 'em, she had no one to play with, and so she took the punishment herself. She could feel the flesh rippin', the blood tricklin' from the wound and down her skin. Riley watched as the girl squirmed with discomfort, but watchin' wasn't enough; he needed to hear it. "Love hurts sometimes, doesn't it, Peyton?"

"Yes, Mr. Creeper."

Riley laughed. "Please, call me Riley."

"Yes, sir."

"Peyton." He raised his voice ever so slightly. "I told you to call me Riley." The girl writhed in agony now; it was too much. Her hand darted to Riley's wrist. "Oh dear, Peyton," he said disappointedly. "Oh dear."

"No, please–" she cried, pain etched on her pretty face, evident in her dulcet voice. But it was too late. Riley gently lifted the blade from Peyton's thigh; crimson danced along the metal as it glimmered in the basement's light, and spilled effortlessly from the thin cut he'd traced across her leg. He took the doll closest to him in his grasp, and contorted his face as he wrenched the plastic head from the body. "I'm so sorry," the girl sobbed quietly, tears streamed down her face as she fell on to her side, mournin' the loss o' Hayley.

"A lesson learnt," Riley spat. Peyton refused to move; she daren't lose another friend. Riley stood and headed for the exit. His twisted smile was the last thing Peyton would see as he turned off the light, left the room, and closed the door behind him, confinin' her to another night in the darkness.

4

You have every right to look upon the man who's filled your glasses all night with such disdain. Mr. Riley Creeper; one sick and twisted son o' a whore.

See, you thought Gina was bad. But at least she didn't bring harm to the kids she took in. In fact, she probably gave 'em a better lifestyle than the one they were used to. They got their fix o' *paimacozine*, no questions asked, and they got away with fuckin' murder. Don't get me wrong; I'm not condonin' what that woman done for a single second. But she was a damn saint compared to Riley.

There had been four in total. Georgia Croft was the first, thirteen years o' age, stolen as she walked the streets to school. The next mornin', her parents had stood broken hearted in one o' Riley's gift shops, askin' to put a missin' poster in his window. O' course he agreed; but not before suggestin' darkly that maybe the rumours o' the Eight-Til-Late were true. They just said it was more likely that the asshole kids at school had gone too far this time. Poor girl lasted less than a week before Riley took her breakfast one mornin' and found her swingin' from a wooden beam in the basement. Note to self; don't leave a homesick suicidal teenager alone in a basement with fishin' equipment and a stool. So, what do you do with a dead body, when the police are scourin' ditches, rivers and the likes expectin' to find her face down and breathless?

You dump it outside the Eight-Til-Late, o' course.

To my mind, there's only one thing worse than a child snatcher; and that's a child snatcher with a fuckin' brain in their God damn head. See, Riley reckoned, what with the stories o' Gina turnin' kids into zombies gainin' prominence, a child could go missin' and everybody would assume it was her. So when Nicholas Shelvey, Thomas Keene and Peyton Adams disappeared within a few days o' each other, the general belief was that Gina's army had grown; no one suspected it could possibly be the kindly toy shop owner down the street.

And I'll bet Riley was smilin' to himself at that fact as he served pasta sauce on to five tiny dishes in his kitchen, listenin' to Mia Bellezza on the record player.

I guess you're wonderin' why her name keeps croppin' up so often.

See, Mia Bellezza was a famous Italian singer from years back, and she was a goddess. Long black hair, eyes the colour o' honey, full red lips, and a slender frame complimented by beautiful evenin' gowns whenever she performed on stage. She had a few minor hits in her home country usin' her native tongue, but then she releases a track in English and suddenly she's a household name around the globe. Everythin' she sang was a phenomenon. People were goin' crazy for her; some were even obsessed, like our very own Mr. Creeper. Got his hands on as much Mia Bellezza merchandise as he could. Albums, singles, lunchboxes, pencil cases. Even went to great lengths to own a limited edition signed poster, spent a ridiculous sum o' money if you ask me. He lived, slept and breathed Mia Bellezza. So when he found out she'd married an English entrepreneur called Thomas Underwood, and named their only child Nicholas, o' course Riley wanted a Thomas and a Nicholas o' his own.

And Peyton? She was just unfortunate to have long black hair and honey coloured eyes, is all.

Riley takes the dishes down the hall on a trolley, unlocks the first door and sees that Nicholas is no longer seated, but facin' the corner o' the room. Riley enters and places the dish in the centre o' the room, exits and locks the door. In the second room, he finds Thomas lyin' silently on his side with the television off. In the basement, Peyton has evidently tried to put her doll back together again without success. Riley touches her hair lightly and smiles, places her dish in her hands, so she needn't struggle to find it when the door closes and leaves her in the dark. He turns his attention to Ladonna now, carryin' the remainin' two plates up to her room.

"Dinner time," he announces as he slips inside. Ladonna opens her left eye weakly, wants to eat but doesn't wanna move. Riley puts the food on the end o' the bed and helps her sit up, puts a plate on her lap and starts to eat his own. She just stares at the pasta. "Eat up. It's your favourite." She stays just starin' at it for a little while, and Riley gets agitated watchin' her, so he helps. Let's just say he's a little rough, tryna feed her quicker than she's capable o' eatin', and she ends up with more round her mouth than actually in it, she lets him know that and it only frustrates him more.

"I cook the food, I serve the food, I'll damn well eat it for you too, shall I?" And he launches the plate against the wall. Ladonna doesn't move, he's done this before, she knows he'll calm down soon. And he does, gives her the same old apology, says he overreacted, says he forgets that she can't always do things for herself, it just upsets him that she's not as able as she once was. And then he wipes food from her lips, watches her breathe, touches her cheek, touches her hair. She brushes him away weakly; irritable, but not strong enough to get him off.

He tries to kiss her mouth, but she turns her head. He kisses her cheek, licks her skin, down to her neck and she groans. His hand is inside her robe now, she lets it happen, just for a few seconds before she musters every ounce remainin' to grab him by the wrist and pull it from her flesh. But this only turns Riley on more, and he's butt fuckin' naked within seconds, and he's slappin' his piece at Ladonna's face. She bears her teeth, catches his prick with an incisor but he doesn't register this as pain, no, only pleasure; and then he grabs hold o' Ladonna and turns her over, she's makin' all sorts o' noises and kickin' her legs as hard as she can, but Riley always found that this only made removin' her underwear easier. And then with his hands rough on her hips, he eases himself deep inside her. She's got silent tears in her eyes, and she makes her disapproval known, she always does, but Riley only hears the soft sweet voice o' Mia Bellezza.

Hold me like you've held no other,
Love me like I'm your first lover.
Whisper those sweet nothings through the night.
Kiss me expertly and yet,
As though no other lips you've met.
And still be mine this time come morning light.

He doesn't last long, he never does; collapses in a sweaty heap on Ladonna's back, waits until his breathin' has calmed, then slides out and slips into his boxer shorts. Picks up his trousers, rummages through a pocket, takes out Ladonna's medication and tosses it on the bed beside her, as though it's payment and she's nothin' more than a whore.

"Clean yourself up," he says before leavin' the room. Ladonna looks at the tablet, wonders why she should take it, if this is her life now. Regrets that decision years ago, certainly. But this is her punishment, she decides, and grabs at the capsule. She eyeballs the glass o' water, but takes it down dry.

The Brief Interlude

"You're not right in the head," Fitz said, sipping the tip of his drink, then slowly edging the glass away from his mouth. "I wanted you to give us a little home truth about the man, not slander. Tell me he went to a Bellezza concert and got caught with his hands in the knicker drawer; but don't call him a paedophile rapist just to get your own back. The list I make of your wrongdoings just grew a shade darker."

"Wait a second," The Bastard replied, his voice evidently more than annoyed. "You think I'd amend my retellin' o' the past for the sake o' vengeance? Not a chance! If I wanted to get back at Riley, I'd just shove my foot in his ass and bust open his functional eye; either that, or tell this story just how it happened, which is what I'm doin'. Besides, if I started makin' stuff up now, no doubt Mr. Publishin' House and his four-eyed sidekick would notice some discrepancies in the timeline. I'd be runnin' the risk o' possible inconsistencies; one second, poor little Timmy's a skinny orphaned boy with no education, the next he's a biology graduate who owns a gym and knows how to build a firearm."

"I'm glad you mention that," Fitz mused. The Bastard glared at him indignantly.

"And why's that? 'Cause little Timmy's rags to riches tale o' revenge is more appealin' to you?"

"Not at all. I just wondered how Mr. Creeper came to run this pub, when all his time and energy seems devoted to the gift shops and his 'family'."

The Bastard slammed his fists down in anger.

"I was gettin' to that, you impatient fuck!" Paul took a silent gulp of his drink. "Every guy wants to run their own bar, right? A place for the guys and girls to convene for a drink or two and a laugh, whenever they want. Well, Riley was no different. See, back when this tale is set, Riley was just another customer, and it was run by this foulmouthed foreigner called Christoph, a beast o' a guy who thought he could get away with murder, until murder done away with him instead. Rumours had started spreadin' about Riley's close relationship with Ladonna; y'know, proper playground crap, guys makin' up stories down the pub for fun, and startin' a new conversation whenever the victim comes within earshot, pretendin' like they're all best buds. And Riley had no idea he was the subject o' one o' the rumours, until one day he said to me: 'I'm gonna be the boss here someday.' And I just laughed as he looked about the place, his drunken head rollin' around on his shoulders. Then his eyes locked with the barman.

'Hey, Chris! Why'd you name this place The Finger Inn?'

And Christoph, see, he wasn't any good at bein' subtle, he always had to be the last in line when it came to Chinese whispers. 'Becuss I herd zat before you fuck your muzzer, you get her vet by sticking ze finger in.' It took a couple o' seconds, but then everybody got the joke and burst out laughin'. Riley just narrowed his eyes and drank from his bottle. Then he leaned in close to me, so that I'd hear him over the roar o' the others. 'I'm gonna kill that S.O.B., and I'm gonna be the boss here someday.' And then he stood up and left the pub; and true to his word, the next time Riley walked through those doors, he was the boss."

"How?"

"'Cause Christoph was the centrepiece o' another rumour flyin' around. Guy had himself a *paimacozine* addiction so bad that he was pawnin' his assets daily to fund his stash. Riley cut him a deal; sign over The Finger Inn, and not only would he let Christoph remain behind the bar, but he'd increase his *Kool Kidz* product supply for the shop, and direct 'em to Christoph, free o' charge. Satisfy both their urges. Christoph signs the contract. Riley gives him a can o' *Kool Kidz* alcohol, laden with *paimacozine*. Before the liquid can spill from the tin and into Christoph's eager mouth, Riley shoots him in the chest."

"And just that like, he owns his own pub?"

"Just like that, he expands his business. Got the contract to prove it, too."

"And no one wondered where Christoph disappeared to?"

"O' course people wondered! But the new barmaid with the big tits tells you he moved back home and signed the lease over to Riley Creeper; and suddenly you don't care anymore."

Fitz gave a short laugh. "So what happened next?" he asked. "With Ladonna and the kids?"

"Oh, you're done?" The Bastard snorted. "Do I have permission to continue my story?" He picked up Fitz's glass and helped himself to another mouthful of ale.

"We'll add theft to that list, shall we?"

"You interrupt one o' my tales again, and you'll be addin' *mur*."

"What the fuck is *mur*?"

"It's *murder*; but you'll be dead before the second syllable escapes that cocksuckin' mouth o' yours."

Behind the blue curtain, Riley caressed the hand puppet and smiled to himself.

Tale 4

$M_r.$ C_{reeper} $_{(part}$ $II_)$

5

Do you remember your playground days?

How every school had that one weird kid, whose life you assumed was truly awful? Maybe they used to flinch every time somebody walked too near, or the only verbal response you got from 'em was a screech, as though social interaction was new to 'em; they would usually sit by themselves, only a few metres from a great horde o' friends and read a book, occasionally expressin' their distaste at the level o' noise by scrunchin' up their face and scrapin' their chair irritably.

Did you ever consider that to their mind *you* were the weird kid? And that their own life was perfectly normal? See, that was Riley. Any outsider with the tiniest shred o' a brain cell could tell he wasn't all right upstairs. Three captive children and an incestuous relationship with his dear old mother? Christ on a bike, the kid had more issues than the old Batman comics. But Riley didn't see it that way at all. He had three lovin' little ones to look after, and a really close bond with the woman who had brought him up; life was great. And let's face it, he was gettin' pussy all the time, what's not to love about that life?

But all good things must come to an end, right?

I think it had somethin' to do with Georgia's death. That's it; people were beginnin' to question why she hadn't made the cut. Why she had been the only one to turn up dead; and I mean properly dead, not *undead*. Why wasn't she good enough for Gina? And then some started to dismiss Gina's involvement altogether, that someone else had been involved, and when the girl took her own life they panicked, didn't know what to do, left her outside the Eight-Til-Late so fingers would point at Gina.

79

But now the fingers were startin' to point elsewhere. Accusations were flyin' everywhere, and truly, it tore this town apart. Neighbours who were once friends now avoided each other in the streets, or offered 'em a false smile before rushin' off to their loved ones to pour gas into the fire.

"Mr. Peterson up the road has got the shifty eyes of a pervert."

"Have you seen the size of Eddie's scar? I bet Georgia gave that to him."

"That Mr. Creeper is always around kids; I wouldn't be surprised if Peyton was locked away in his basement as we speak."

"I've always had reservations about that Creeper."

Riley had overheard a few remarks; especially when the old women, who had never quite grasped the concept o' whisperin', had stood waggin' chins in the corner o' one o' his shops, buyin' their milk and mornin' papers. He'd greet 'em as he always did, and they'd respond in kind, but when his back was turned to straighten up the magazine rack, they'd be gossipin' the possibility o' Riley's involvement in the disappearances. And the more gossip he heard, the more Riley felt like a fly on the web o' a fast approachin' spider.

And then one evenin', just as Riley was about to lock up the bar, things came to a fuckin' end, and then some.

6

I was sat in this very chair and watched as a couple o' guys staggered through those doors and to the bar. Riley told 'em politely enough to be on their way, but they were adamant that their night wasn't over; they said somethin' about bein' thrown outta The Pelican, else they wouldn't be in such a shit heap as The Finger Inn. Well, Riley didn't take too kindly to that now, did he? Told this pair o' assholes to get lost with a little less civility the second time round. And they were about ready to throw some punches, until I made my voice heard; remind you o' anyone? Anyways, they got the message, loud and clear. But they weren't leavin' without a partin' shot.

"Stick your fucking pub up your arse, you paedophile cunt."

No one's ever gonna be thrilled to be labelled either o' those things, never mind both in the same breath. Riley's made o' pretty stern stuff, but given the circumstances, I think it's fair to say he left The Finger Inn in a pretty foul mood after knockin' back some o' the good shit. Creeper staggers home; struggles with his keys at first, enters and climbs the staircase, unsteady on his feet. Still swiggin' from the neck squeezed in his fist, he sees Ladonna sat on the edge o' her bed, sweatin' like a fat kid in a sauna.

"You're awake," he says, matter-o'-factly.

"I heard it again."

"I told you to stay in bed." One more time. "I told you to stay in bed!" And he smashes the bottle against the mantelpiece, shattered shards dance across the floorboards as precious alcohol slides down the wall and forms in pools at Riley's feet. Ladonna had seen this enough times, watched as Riley's mood turned foul, aggressive, sexually aggressive, and ended in apologies; but this time she finally snapped.

"What the fuck is wrong with you?" She says it so suddenly, so spiteful, it takes Riley by shock and he stops dead in his tracks, eyes frozen to Ladonna's and mouth hangin' open with no words ready to leap from within. "You make me sick. That poor family. Not a day goes by without thinking of that poor woman, staring at an empty school uniform, wondering what became of her son. And then I stop to consider that maybe I'd done them a favour. You make me sick. You are nothing like my Edward. You were a fucking mistake. I should've left you at the hospital."

"You don't mean that."

Ladonna just stares back at him, unflinchin'.

"Oh I do. I mean every word of it and more. You were a filthy, fucking mistake, and I should've left you at the hospital with your–"

"Don't say it."

"I should've left you at the hospital with them and never looked back."

"No! No! No!" Riley cannot bear to hear Ladonna's words, like knives tearin' pieces from his pulsatin' heart.

"You don't think there were days when I wanted to give you back? Make it right? But it never would be right, would it? Nobody could truly forgive that! If God gave me back my boy right now, I could never forgive Him for taking him away in the first place. You are nothing like my Edward; you were a fucking mistake, and I should've just left you at the hospital with your real parents!"

"Shut the fuck up!" Riley pushes her hard in the chest and she stumbles backwards on to the bed. Her breaths become short and sharp, pain paints itself on her face. "You think you're better than me? You're the one who made me what I am today!"

"Riley, help–"

"Shut the fuck up, child snatcher."

See, Ladonna wasn't Riley's real mother. His real parents had last seen him when he was just seven years old, lyin' unconscious on a hospital bed after a fight in the playground. Bruises up and down his arms and legs, and a nasty gash on the side o' his head where he took a fall and hit a rock. Doctor said he'd come round in no time at all. Daddy goes to fetch some hot drinks, while Mommy makes a call to let the family know their precious Riley is all right; meanwhile, a couple o' wards away, an inconsolable Ladonna has heard her own son's heart monitor deliver that soul destroyin' beep, seen the sheets pulled up over his head, smelt the fuckin' lavender fragrance o' the nurse's uniform as she tried to ease the pain with a firm embrace, but no amount o' hugs will end this sufferin', no. Ladonna came to the hospital with a son, and she was gonna *leave* the hospital with a son. She staggers away, drunk on grief, eyes on every bed as she goes. Children surrounded by parents, grandparents, even siblin's; and then there's Riley. It happens in an instant. Before she knows it, she's lowerin' him into the rear o' her car. Drivin' away, she swears she hears the sound o' a mother screamin', but she doesn't go back, it's too late now. Riley remembers his eyes openin'; the fear o' lookin' up at Ladonna. How the tables had turned all these years later.

Ladonna's hands shoot to the dressin' gown pocket, panic when she doesn't feel the box, the pocket's empty, where's the medicine, the pocket's empty.

"Pill," she says weakly. Her eyes bear deeply into Riley's, but his response is somewhat vacant. She glances around frantically, sees a box o' tablets on the chest o' drawers, aims a fragile finger. Riley looks to where she's pointin', but he doesn't move. She fails at gettin' to her feet, she is weak, succeeds in only fallin' to the floor. Her breathin' gets even shorter, even sharper, she's dyin', she knows she's dyin' and she knows she'll be dead soon when blood starts to rise in her throat and her breaths become less like breaths and more like gentle gags, red spills down her chin with every tiny pulse her useless heart can muster, before she chokes her last. Riley continues to stare at her for a short while, emotionless. And then he sits down on the edge o' her bed. And then he turns on the television.

7

And Riley watched that television set for quite some time. He grabbed himself a beer and put one o' his Mia Bellezza video tapes in the machine, watched as though he hadn't a care in the world, as though the woman he had cooked and cleaned for the majority o' his adult life hadn't just died before the bed on which he sat, as though today had been a good day for Mr. Riley Creeper.

But somethin' happens to that man as he sits there watchin' the television, sits there watchin' Mia Bellezza glide across the stage, purrin' her every word. See, he starts caressin' the neck o' his bottle like he's jerkin' off, and before long his prick is so firm in his pants that he just can't sit comfortably any more, and he reaches one hand in there, has an awkward tug, pulls his pants down to his ankles, drops to his knees and starts gratifyin' himself with a little more ease this time. And he goes to work on himself nice and slow, one eye on the television, one eye on his junk, and one eye on the box o' tissues, if you catch my drift. But suddenly he isn't so content with just doin' it himself; especially when he knocks his beer all over Ladonna's body, his drunken frame o' mind puts two and two together and decides he can get this dead bitch wet enough to fuck.

So he starts tearin' away at her clothes, and he's kissin' her skin all over, flicks his tongue over her saggy tits, guides his mouth down her leather body; and then he's spittin' on his hands and rubbin'

82

her downstairs, I swear he's playin so hard that he damn near burns the lips right off the poor bitch. A couple o' times he forces himself inside, but it doesn't feel right. No, Riley remembers what he enjoyed most about fuckin' Ladonna when she was alive; the struggle. O' course, she was too drugged up most o' the time to raise a real fight, but the notion o' authority was important to Riley. He wanted to be loved, but he wanted to be feared in equal measure; he wanted love to be spawned o' hate, much like his own feelin's towards Ladonna. He could recall a time when he used to despise the very essence o' that woman, but look at him now; tryna will her pussy back from the dead for one last moment o' glory.

No, this will not do.

What Riley needed was the fight; fuckin' Ladonna now was too easy, what Riley needed was the fight, the struggle, the love, the fear, the only way he knew how. A grin slowly stretches wide on Riley's face, as he pulls his prick free from his parent. He climbs to his feet, staggers down the staircase, stares aimlessly at three doors; and I believe he feigns deliberation before headin' to the basement.

8

It's quiet; she acknowledges this fact, as the soft, rhythmic tickin' from the clock on the wall is the only sound she hears. She wonders then, just how long it had been that way; that no other sound had entered her head for as long as she could remember. She turns her head, and looks at the man lyin' next to her, his breathin' silent and steady. She's sure they spoke that day, but she doesn't remember what his voice sounds like. Nor her own, for that matter. She knew she should be cryin'; but no tears had left Nancy Shelvey's eyes since the police stopped lookin' for her son. It didn't feel right. And now she felt nothin' at all.

She wasn't sure why she climbed outta bed and padded barefoot down the staircase for a glass o' water. Maybe it was an inability to sleep; maybe it was a thirst she couldn't feel, but was aware it should be present. But whatever reason it was, she was thankful, that's for certain. Thankful that, from the window, she saw the figure cross the lawn. A hand tapped gently against the door, and Nancy dropped her glass. It shattered upon the wooden floor, stabbed at her feet, but she felt no pain. Tremblin', she approached the door. Had she still been in bed, she wouldn't have seen him, wouldn't have believed it possible. Had she still been in bed, she wouldn't have heard the soft knockin', or possibly dismissed it as the wind. Had she still been in bed, she wouldn't have opened the door to find young Nicholas stood there, nor would she have screamed and cried and felt everythin' once again and all at once.

"My baby!" And she held him closer than anythin' else in the world. Damn near squeezed the oxygen from the boy's lungs, she pulled him in so tight. "Who did this to you?" His hair was scruffy, shirt torn, jeans a muddy mess. His face had bled and dried, and the boy glanced up as his dad appeared at the foot o' the staircase, approached in shock, knelt and held his wife and only child.

"Who did this Nicholas?" he asked, his voice crackin' with sorrow, elation, anger, everythin'. "Who did this?" The boy hadn't spoken for so long, he barely recognized the voice that escaped his lips himself.

"Creeper."

9

Peyton could recall the first time light had crept into her prison. Darkness had been the only thing she'd seen for what seemed like a lifetime; and then wooden steps came slowly into view as a door above her creaked open, the light from Riley's house a dim torch peerin' into her abode from a distance enough to make her shield her eyes in pain. And then the pull o' the light switch, the bulb above suddenly flickerin' into life, the feelin' as though she was being burned by the sun pressin' down on her. She had screamed, and so Mr. Creeper had broken one o' her dolls. Every visit thereafter, Peyton tried her best not to make a sound, but it'd been a hell o' a struggle. Some days he would only provide her with food and drink; these were easy days. Others, he wanted interaction, and so he'd pet her long hair and whisper songs into her ear. His touch, even his breath upon her skin, made her very apprehensive, and Riley knew that. And so, his touch had been gettin' firmer o' late. Or rather, more aggressive. The knife incident, well; that had been the nastiest to date. Peyton never imagined it could get any worse.

Her eyes opened as soon as she heard the door above squeak, adjusted slowly to the light that began pourin' in. Peyton looked at her toys; heads and bodies lay strewn across the dirty floor, but she gripped little Stephanie tight behind her back. Mr. Creeper's footsteps got unsteadily louder, closer. She decided not to look towards him, but could feel his stare, every step o' the way, and then he stopped a step or two before her. Peyton squeezed her eyes shut tight, waitin' for somethin' to happen, anythin'; but nothin' did for a minute or two. Riley just looked. Cast his gaze upon her long black hair, down her delicate face, over her ragged clothes. And then he reaches down slowly. Brushes her cheek lightly.

"Look at me." Peyton initially refuses; but she knows she will have to offer him a glance sooner rather than later if her friend is gonna survive the night. "Look at me." She prises open one honey coloured eye, and he smiles. "My beautiful girl." Runs a hand through her hair. "Mia." Down her face, squeezes her shoulder. "I've dreamed o' this moment for so long." The poor girl starts to shiver. Riley turns and walks away slowly, and Peyton wonders for a moment what he is doin'. Hears mumbled words, sees fumbled movements. And then she realises he is singin'. And then she realises he is naked.

You take me to the highest heights,
When you take my hand and dim the lights.
You put me on those clouds above,
When you give me your love.
You take me to that hallowed place,
Where the only rain is upon my face.
You fit me like a hand in a glove,
When you give me your love.

Peyton was sure she'd felt pure terror before, but nothin' compared to the fear she felt now as Riley turned to face her, a smile across his face, and a body part in his hand that she hadn't known existed. It was this element o' the unknown that scared her the most, associated it only with Bad, and had Stephanie not been in such pristine condition she woulda screamed to her heart's content, for sure.

But fortunately, she never had to.

A noise from overhead froze Riley to the spot. The sound o' the front door bein' sent from its hinges, followed by the cries o' angry men, had him back in his clothes in next to no time.

"Where the fuck are you, Creeper?"

Riley looked at Peyton.

"Not a sound from you, remember?" he snarled menacin'ly, and then he snatched the girl up into his arms, and cautiously climbed the stairs. Peerin' carefully round the doorframe, he saw two men ascendin' the stairs towards Ladonna's room, and a third enterin' what was Nicholas' cell.

"Are you here, Tommy?" one o' them yelled.

"Shit! There's a dead body up here!"

"Check the other rooms, they're around here somewhere!"

It took four kicks o' a size nine boot before Thomas' door was sent flyin' open.

"There's a boy in here! What's your name, son?" The man disappeared inside. Riley seized his chance. He ran for the front door with Peyton over his shoulder. The sound o' his hurried feet alerted everyone in the house. One man stayed with Thomas while the others pursued. A bullet smacked the wood o' the door as Riley realised they were armed. Women were waitin' on the front lawn and they screamed as Riley charged past 'em, grabbed their shoes and began throwin' 'em, anythin' that could be used as a weapon would be. But Riley avoided anythin' that came his way, just kept movin', wasn't sure where to go, just had to move. And then more people, fast approachin', some in cars, some with flashin' lights, policemen.

Riley kept movin', tried to stay outta the light, tried to move in the shadows. But he could hear the cries from behind gettin' closer, could feel their munitions landin' closer, they could see his every move; so he kept headin' away from town, found himself movin' towards the bridge, knew where he would try to shelter, the gift shops, it had to be, the gift shops. And so he got there as fast as he could, no time to find the key in his pockets, no time to fumble with the lock, he just smashed his fist right through the glass and pulled it open that way, threw Peyton inside and tried to barricade the entrance as best he could. But o' course they'd find a way in, a fuckin' desk wasn't gonna stop a bloodthirsty mob from gettin' in and tearin' the man limb from limb.

So Riley did the only thing his panickin' brain could think to tell him to do.

He started the fire.

10

Two things went through Riley's head as he watched the people outside jump back from the flames. 'That did the trick,' was no doubt the first, as the fire licked the gas and danced along wood, formin' a blisterin' wall in the doorway and in front o' the large glass display window, which incidentally wasn't there for too much longer.

The second was a bullet.

It caught Riley just above the ear, and tore a small chunk right out the side o' his head, sent him flyin' backwards in agony as bricks and wood and all sorts o' shit was thrown through the flames in his direction. Riley began cursin' violently, and throwin' cabinets o' ornaments around like a madman, and if Peyton wasn't scared enough already she sure as fuck was by this point. See, the fire; it just spreads, eatin' every piece o' plastic it touches, swings from the curtains and climbs the walls. Riley watches it with a mixture o' awe and fear, as it consumes everythin' he had worked for his entire life.

"Give us the girl, you sick fuck!" he could hear amongst the yells outside, as desperate, angry people began to take out their anger on surroundin's; tearin' up bins and the like for makeshift missiles, even tried gettin' the bus shelter up outta the ground, but they only succeeded in pullin' it over and shatterin' the glass. Frustration was taken out on anythin' and everythin', wishin' instead it was Riley they were beatin' to the ground. "Give us the fucking girl!"

Riley turns to face her. Poor little Peyton.

"Oh yes," Riley says. "The fuckin' girl." And he laughs. "Ain't nobody here gonna save you this time." And he jumps forward, pounces on her.

In her shock at his sudden movement she loses her grip on her doll, watches as it flies through the air and lands beside the fire. It takes a matter o' seconds for the sheer heat o' the flames to do the damage; Peyton begins to shake violently, manages to free herself from Riley's grasp as her limbs strike out at him, as her doll's face turns to liquid and melts to the wooden floor.

"I didn't make a sound!" she screams. "This never should have happened! You're a bad man, I didn't make a sound!" And then she screams and screams as loud as she can, almost as though tryin' to justify little Stephanie's demise. It's Riley's turn to be stunned, as the girl swings her arms at him, catches him in the face, fingernails claw deep into his eye, and he screams as he blindly shoves her to the ground. She gets to her feet and charges forward to hit him some more. Riley doesn't know how to handle it; he grabs a metal bar to protect himself, the fuckin' coward. The metal is red hot in his grasp, and he drops it no sooner has he picked it up, cries in pain.

Peyton collides into him, they hit the wall hard and send the shelves crashin' down on top o' them, trappin' 'em both. The fire begins to creep closer towards 'em, and Riley, dazed, cannot push the girl off. His mouth is fillin' with blood, seems most o' his teeth got knocked out as they landed heavy. The shop is a mass o' smoke by now, and they both start coughin' as the flames flirt dangerously near their skin, sweat is slidin' down Riley's face as he musters every ounce o' strength to roll Peyton and the shelves away and clamber to his feet. Riley looks down with one eye at the girl, blood is pourin' from a head wound where the wood had caught her, her chest is risin' and fallin' rapidly as she fights for air while smoke fills her lungs, and for a second he sees Ladonna. She was right. No mother could truly forgive someone for stealin' their child. Even if he gave the girl back, there was no way Riley would survive the night. It was too late to save this. It had to end here. He took the girl in his arms, and carried her into the fire.

T_{he} F_{inal} T_{ale}

"I hate the way he tells that story." Riley's voice startled the travellers, sounding so suddenly from behind them. "He always kills me off at the end." He slowly walked back to his bar.

"You deserve to be dead, you sick fuck," Paul growled beneath his breath, and he slammed his drink down so fiercely that a crack formed on the underside of the glass, a thin trickle of ale escaping along the wood. Three pairs of eyes darted hastily towards his direction; Fitz placed a hand on his friend's shoulder.

"Paul?" he asked, perplexed by the sudden fury radiating from such a usually placid man. "Calm down, yeah?"

Paul shot him a foul stare.

"Calm down?" he replied, his voice still barely above a whisper. He shrugged Fitz's hand away. "You've been sitting there all this time, writing your notes with your blood boiling because of a few clichés; I dare to voice my disgust at the child molester who's been topping our glasses all night with a smile, and you tell me to calm down? What the hell is wrong with you?"

"Have you not learned one thing from this evening?" Fitz hissed in response. "Every word to have escaped that bastard's lips has been fabricated. Riley is about as much a kiddie snatcher as you or I are! If you believe that last story for one second, then you're telling me that you believe in ghosts, and zombies, and Father fucking Christmas."

"Maybe you're just too stubborn to admit that you believe it yourself," The Bastard interrupted. "There's no middle ground in that head o' yours, is there? Everythin' has to be entirely true, or entirely false. You said it yourself; 'cause the fear resides in the not knowin' for sure, does it not, Mr. Fitz?"

"You don't think I have anxieties? Sure I do, just like everybody else. Mainly to do with trust."

"No fuckin' surprises there."

"My whole life has been built on failed relationships. You don't think that the same thought flashes through my mind every time someone feeds me those three little words of affection? Everyone who has ever said that they love me was surely lying. Where are they now? Lying in bed with someone else, or lying alone beneath the ground."

"You think dyin' makes 'em love you any less?"

"Sure it does. The dead feel nothing. But me? I'm alive; I feel everything. Death leads to dejection, rejection to despair. I know another "I love you" will come, and I know there's good a chance that I won't believe it. But what if it's Amy who says it? The thought that I won't believe the words from my own daughter's mouth scares the shit out of me. But the words from your own, Bastard? I have never been more certain in my life that the sentiments you've expressed are complete bullshit."

"You don't think there's even a slight possibility that the last tale was true?" Paul announced. "You heard The Bastard; Riley broke a promise, so The Bastard got even."

"Oh, please! Tales of revenge are always full of fabrication! You ever wonder why no one lets Rick from work borrow their stationery? He stole my lunch from the fridge once, so I told them that he likes to stick pens up his arse after he shits. Does Rick shit? For sure; who doesn't? Does he fornicate himself with a biro before he pulls his pants back up? How the fuck should I know? But I very much doubt it. Fiction spawned of fact got me even, and it got The Bastard even, too."

"Calling someone a child abuser is a little different, don't you think? Who in their right mind would make up something like that about somebody else?"

"These motherfuckers right here, for sure! I have no trouble believing that Riley has a weird obsession with some Italian chick; the jukebox is testament to that. But a kid abductor who fucks his own mother figure? Not a chance! Hell, I'd wager money that Mr. Creeper here bats for the other team; either that, or he's a virgin."

The Bastard let out a little laugh.

"Don't think I've forgotten about you," Fitz continued, turning his attention again to The Bastard. "Yeah, I think I've got you all figured out. All this talk of bad fathers. I reckon it's a guilty conscience. Riley tells us that you never knew Daddy, but tell me this; did your child ever know you?" The Bastard immediately glared at Riley.

"What the fuck have you told 'em?"

"I told 'em nothin', Hanson, I promise you that. Seems Mr. Muscle Man here jus' called your bluff." The Bastard slowly turned to face Fitz, whose grin was as wide as his mouth would allow.

"You think you're so fuckin' smart, don't you?"

"That's where you're wrong," Fitz replied. "People like yourself *think* that you're smart; and people like me, we *know* it. Intelligence isn't something we're born with; we have to earn it. Every day presents opportunities to nurture it; and while you're too busy thinking that you're as gifted as you could possibly be, I'm acknowledging ways in which I can improve."

"Jesus Christ." The Bastard rolled his eyes theatrically. "Four drinks inside o' him, and the humble becomes the egotist. Does he always get like this? One minute, his speech is expletive ridden ignorance; the next, he be *so* eloquent and profound."

"Would it kill you to change your way of life?"

"No, it would not, dear preacher; nor will it make me feel any more alive. Both life and death lie at the bottom o' my glass. I don't get thrills outta anythin' anymore; the closest I can get is the brief satisfaction that comes with a drop o' alcohol. A lifetime o' which has effectively killed me. I'm stuck in a rut; you won't ever see me outside o' these four walls. I live and die at The Finger Inn. You're both lucky enough to still have the chance to escape. Why don't you take it?"

"Because that's what I need right now," Paul retorted. "A lecture from an alcoholic and his paedophile sidekick."

"I resent that word, Four Eyes," Riley said fiercely. "Take it back, else I might start me another fire tonight." He spoke so darkly that it sent a shiver down even Fitz's spine; but Paul refused to be deterred, instead rising from his chair and stepping a few paces towards the barman.

"Pardon fucking me, Saint Creeper!" he yelled as he stood. "You see, where I'm from, stealing kids from their families and using them for sexual gratification is greatly frowned upon. Judging by Hanson's tales, seems the residents of Kramusville feel the same way as I do. If you're not a depraved child molester, pray tell, just what are you?"

A silence more unnerving had never befell the travellers until now; Hanson and Fitz watched as Paul and Riley eyeballed each other with such disdain for the others' existence that it seemed as though a mere blink could cause bodily harm. Finally, Riley responded.

"What 'bout you, Paul?"

"Excuse me?"

"Seems we know a li'l somethin' 'bout everyone present but you. What's your story?"

"I don't think so—"

"You said it yourself," The Bastard interrupted. "It's too late for new characters; let's hear about one we're more acquainted with."

"Whose side are you on?" Paul growled.

"I don't choose sides. Not anymore. There was a time when Hanson might've; but now I am just a bastard drunk. My bed's been made, and so I lie in it. That's the way my story goes. Question is, Paul; who's gonna tell the story o' your life?"

"That son of a bitch stole the innocence from helpless little children, and broke a so-called sacred pact between the two of you. Moments ago, you wanted to wring his neck; and yet, now all you want to do is hear about my rural upbringing! Well you know what? Fuck you! You're not just a shit storyteller; you're a shit audience, too."

"And you're not?"

"Meaning?"

"I know a skeleton lurks in your closet; 'cause you've heard things, Paul, and it is quite clear that you haven't been listenin'."

Paul suddenly appeared stunned. "You know nothing about my past."

"I know enough to be certain that you're hidin' somethin'. You're not a family man, are you, Paul? You had your chances, but somethin' held you back. Your attention to your friend's relationship, the way you almost father him; certainly suggests to me that you don't wanna see Fitz here make the same mistakes as you did."

"Get fucked."

"And that as a response just tells me I've hit the nail on the head. What was it that drove you and your wife to divorce, Paul? What caused you to miss out on your little man's upbringin'? Why did Riley's story upset you so goddamn much? Do you see how easily the dots can be connected if you just pay attention? What childhood memory have you tried to repress so desperately that it's affected your relationship with children ever since? What did you see, Paul, o' which you denied to speak? What did you hear, o' which you refused to listen?"

The Bastard leaned in really close. "Why do you flinch every time I say the word *bill*?" Paul screwed his face up tight, and felt the burn of all eyes upon him, as the others waited with bated breath for his response; he weakly cleared his throat.

"He was just a little boy back then," he said quietly, his voice taut, almost broken as he fought back the tears that threatened to slide down his blushing cheeks. "He didn't deserve it, no one deserves that. I was too young to know what was happening at the time, that's why I didn't help him." Fitz's mouth fell open in disbelief.

"Paul, what are you–"

"I'd never wanted a brother. Things were just fine the way they were. I didn't want a brother; they knew that; I told them countless times, things were better off left alone. But did they listen? Of course they didn't, they spent the next two years trying everything to conceive again. You know, it felt more like they were going out of their way to piss me off, instead of fulfilling their utopian family dreams. And then, everyone goes crazy for the new kid, gifts come pouring in thick and fast for the newest addition to the family, and what do I get except for constant reminders that I'm the oldest by seven years, I've got to look out for little Billy, be the protective sibling. And I tried, God knows I spent years trying. But that little shit got me into so much trouble crying wolf, that I went right on back to resenting him.

I actually stopped him from stepping out into the road once. Grabbed him hard by the collar, pulled him back before he got hit by a motorbike. He told Mum that I'd hurt him, never mind the fact I'd saved his life, all she saw were the bruises on his neck and the tears in his eyes, and I was sent upstairs with a sore arse and a hungry stomach. And he knew that he could get his way by turning on the waterworks, so that night when…" He paused momentarily to play with the rim of his glass. The pain it caused Paul to recount this event was evident, as he considered his next words, wondered if he had the strength to say them aloud at all.

"You know, you don't have to go on," Fitz said. "Whatever it is you're about to say, it can wait until these two are out of earshot."

"I've spent the whole night tellin' you tales, and you're gonna deny me this one?" The Bastard scoffed. "Where's the justice in that?"

Fitz shot him a steely glare.

"So cry me a fucking river, Miss America. Hey, why don't you buy the guy an ale; even then you might not be so lucky."

"I can still hear…" Paul began, but he trailed off as he removed his glasses and wiped his eyes with a thumb and forefinger. "God, I can still fucking hear him! Crying, screaming, calling out my name; but I just carried on playing with my action figures. It was only when he fell silent that I made my way downstairs."

"Where were your parents?" Fitz asked.

"They were out. Some awards ceremony at my dad's workplace. That's why Uncle Fred was taking care of us."

"So then, where was Uncle Fred?"

Paul couldn't hold it in any longer; he shoved the glass in front of him to the floor and buried his head into his folded arms upon the table.

"I'm gonna need you to compose yourself 'fore you come up for air, Four Eyes," Riley said coolly. "You break one more o' my glasses an' it'll cost you."

"You say one more fucking word, and I'll break more than your precious glass, Creeper," Paul spat through tears. "I've held my silence for too long! Pretended that I hadn't seen Fred's hand over Billy's mouth, that I hadn't watched as he abused his own nephew, that I hadn't looked into my brother's dying eyes as he tried to wrestle free and took a fatal blow to the head. Uncle Fred knew I'd seen everything; that's why he made all those threats afterwards, told me I'd be in big trouble if I ever let slip our little secret. But I'd already forced myself to peer through these same goddamn fingers as he got Billy dressed, smashed his head against the marble fireplace, made it look like he'd taken a fall, stood back to admire his handiwork; that was my real punishment. For not being the protective older sibling that my parents had asked me to be. And I've been blaming myself ever since. No amount of counselling will ever change that. If I'd just done something, *anything*, there's a chance that Billy would've survived that night. And Fred? He could've been punished too, instead of overdosing on his kitchen table before my parents ever knew the truth. People like you and Uncle Fred are all the same, Creeper. Your victims are tortured every single day that they are blessed with opening their eyes, but you? You take the coward's way out because you couldn't handle even a fraction of the shit you subject us to. And for that, you deserve to die. But you don't get to walk into the fire; you should be pushed."

Fitz's expression of shock was still fixated upon his friend, before his head slowly turned to face The Bastard.

"How?" was all he could manage to croak.

"How what?" The Bastard replied, with a great air of assurance.

"You must have some inside knowledge; I'm sure of it, there's no way you could've pulled that out of nowhere! I've known this guy for the best part of my life, and never heard that story before. You've known him all of half a night, so how the fuck would you know about that?"

"What, that Four Eyes here was an accessory to murder? Course I didn't fuckin' know! But it just further serves to prove my point that you boys haven't been payin' attention. I wasn't lookin' for *your* story o' remorse; rather, I was lookin' for *mine*. But the puzzle pieces aren't quite comin' together like they do for others."

"What others?"

"You think you're the first travellers I've entertained with my facts? Forget about it! I've told tales tonight that I've told a thousand times, and no doubt will tell a thousand times more. I've sold stories to you that others haven't bought, and knocked back brandies for anecdotes that you will never hear. But there's one story I always end up tellin'; however, tonight may well prove to be an anomaly in my history as the narrator."

"What the fuck are you talking about?" Fitz raged. "What exactly are we missing here? If this story is so fucking important, why haven't you just told us it already?"

"Because it has followed you in the growin' winds, sang to you at the top o' its lungs, even sat across a table all night; and still you haven't been willin' to embrace it. The torment it serves me to revisit, time and time over, is insurmountable. That's why I never *insist* on tellin' it; but see, I like to think I'm a hospitable host, despite my initial hostility towards newcomers, and if you *knock* on the

94

door to my own closet, I will gladly let you in. As long as you understand that the night ends there."

The travellers exchanged a glance. Fitz appeared slightly bewildered, but Paul looked as though a light bulb had just flicked on inside his head. His mouth hung open slightly, lips trembling; memories from hours ago came flooding back to him suddenly, like an ocean's wave slamming against a rock.

"The voices on the bridge."

The Bastard closed his eyes and leaned back in his chair. A faint smile spread across Riley's lips.

"Well look'e here," the barman said, a familiar jauntiness returning to his voice. "Finally we reach the pinnacle o' this lil gatherin'. It took a lil longer than usual, but the plot will always resurface, regardless o' the narrative. An' jus' what did these voices say, Four Eyes?"

"I don't … I can't remember. Not all of it. Just … *pretty voice*." The barman's eyes widened in delight.

"Pudderwitz," The Bastard growled, slamming his fists down firmly.

"Excuse me?"

"You woulda heard a woman scream too, am I right?" A chill ran down Paul's spine.

"What do you know?"

"I happen to know that the tale you're after concerns a very dear friend o' mine, who went by the name o' Sally Divine."

"And?"

"And I also know that my glass is empty." He shook the empty tumbler between his thumb and forefinger. Paul opened his wallet, and saw that he had no more notes therein.

"Fitz, how much money have you got on you?"

"Enough, but–"

"Buy The Bastard a brandy."

"No way! What's with the sudden urgency? A moment ago you had no interest, almost no recollection of what happened earlier this evening; and yet suddenly it's of paramount importance. Our train will be here within the next hour, we don't need any more stories–"

"Fitz!" The expression of anger etched on Paul's face would stun his friend once more in such a short space of time, coupled with the tone of voice he was using to address him. "I'm not *asking* you, I'm *telling* you, to buy the man a drink! I knew I wasn't going crazy back there! I need to know more about what I heard." He softened now. "Since Billy, I promised myself that if I ever heard a voice cry out in desperation, I'd do something, *anything*. I might not be able to help this Sally, but The Bastard's tale could give me closure. After all I've done for you, do this one thing for me."

Fitz saw a look of sorrow on Paul's face that he'd already seen tonight; upon his own face, staring back from the mirror above Riley's telephone. He ran his hands down his face and sighed.

"Hey, Creeper!" The barman smiled his near toothless grin from behind the bar. "Get your man another brandy. In fact, make it a double. Let's make this last tale the best yet."

Tale 5

*G*ood *O*l' *S*al

1

There's a bar a quarter mile from here, does karaoke every Thursday night. You know why? 'Cause they're fuckin' copycat bastards, that's why! The Finger Inn was doin' the same thing years before the other bar even opened its goddamn doors. Used to pull in quite the crowd, too. A lotta people just turned up to get wasted and watch pissed up pop star wannabes make fools o' 'emselves, but then you had someone every once in a while who could actually hit a note or two.

Could I?

Could I fuck! I could barely hold a glass o' brandy in my hand, let alone hold a fuckin' tune! I never looked at the microphone if I could help it, and the thought o' puttin' it to my open mouth gave me the heebies worse than fingernails on a chalkboard.

And then there was Good Ol' Sal.

2

Now, Sal was a little bit special. See, she could sing, she could dance, and she coulda had every guy eatin' out the palm o' her hand if she'd wanted 'em to. She was a stunner. Had this short brunette hair that she curled up, and a face tainted by not one blemish. Big, beautiful eyes and a perfect mouth, made the voice that came outta it sound even sweeter. Always wore these figure huggin' dresses, too; usually little white numbers, with a feather boa scarf hangin' off her shoulders. And let me tell you, there was a bar full o' men that woulda sold their soul to hang off them shoulders, and sold it twice to hug that figure.

But Sal wasn't interested. Not that she preferred women, or any shit like that. She just wanted to be everybody's friend. And I think that's what made her all the more attractive. Willin' to see the good in everyone. She saw the good in me. Saw the good in Riley somehow, too. Christ knows how, but she did. But not everybody has the good within 'em; it can't be found, no matter how hard you look. Some people are so bad, that even Good Ol' Sal stopped searchin' for their savin' grace.

3

I tried to stay away from this place on Thursday nights. Don't get me wrong, I'm a man who loves his music; but when the songs that you love are bein' brutally murdered, and the songs that you hate are the only ones to be sung by anybody with an ounce o' talent, it does your fuckin' brain in. But I couldn't face the tedium o' nights in front o' the television, or partakin' in activities that I had no interest in whatsoever. There were evenin's at the movies, in the arcades, at the steakhouse. I even tried my hand at bowlin' once, too; but the lure o' alcohol was too strong. I needed it daily, and Thursday wasn't gonna become an exception. And I sure as hell wasn't gonna start drinkin' at some other bar. Too damn loyal to everythin' I love. The Finger Inn, Kramusville, my wife. As much as I liked to get away from my Emily, God rest her soul, I'd never let that woman know hurt 'cause o' somethin' I'd done. Ain't one person in this town who can claim with all honesty to have seen me offer a lady a drink or a ride home. I reckon that's the good in me that Sal saw. 'Cause every other guy was offerin' her drinks and rides like they were goin' outta fashion.

See, Sal used to live in the next town. And she used to walk everywhere, too. Every Thursday, when Riley called for last orders, she'd finish the last o' her soda water and lime, say goodbye to the regulars, politely reject their proposals, and make her way out into the night. Wouldn't even let Riley call her a cab. And she'd walk past Big Joe's recordin' studio, past the Eight-Til-Late on Morgan Avenue, take a right and go by the shoppin' parade, then cross the bridge over the railway tracks. And nobody had a clue if she made it or not until the followin' Thursday, when she'd walk through the door ready for another night on the karaoke machine. Ready for another night o' offers she would kindly refuse.

But there was one person who wasn't prepared to be knocked back. Had the hots for Good Ol' Sal worse than anybody else. Never worked up the courage to talk to her once, until the night he asked her if she wanted a drink.

"No, thank you," she said, with that beautiful smile o' hers. "But you're ever so kind to offer, Mr…" She paused. A look o' guilt spread across her face. "I'm terribly sorry. I don't believe I know your name." What happened next still makes my blood boil to this very day. All he had to do was introduce himself. But the words that escaped his mouth were so vile that I can barely bring myself to repeat 'em. And the way he held her throat like that? Let's just say Peg Leg Pudderwitz was lucky to walk outta The Finger Inn alive that night.

Peg Leg Pudderwitz. Ugliest piece o' shit I've ever laid eyes on. He had this long chiselled face, thin lips curled into a permanent sneer. Big fuck off gap between his two front teeth, pencil moustache stretched messily beneath a crooked nose, with hairs reachin' out from his nostrils. He had one wonky eye, and the other glared out from behind a monocle; he let the string hang loosely down his cheek. And his hair fell like strands o' black straw, unwashed no doubt, unkempt most certainly. Always wore smart clothes, shit dirty mind, but smart all the same; collared shirts, cufflinks that matched the colour o' his tie. Trousers that came right down to his shoe.

That's right; *shoe*.

Singular. Son o' a bitch only had one foot. Why else do you think we called him Peg Leg Pudderwitz? Lost his right leg from the knee down in some accident he never really liked to dwell on. But as much as he didn't like to talk about how he ended up with a wooden limb, he sure as hell liked to let people know he had one. Cut off half a trouser leg o' every fine pair that he owned, just so eyes couldn't help but see his wood. And not the only wood that cocksucker liked to display, if rumours are to be believed. Some reckon he used to whack off under the table throughout Good Ol' Sal's performances, and offer sticky handshakes the rest o' the night. I wouldn't know, I never let that prick touch me, and not just on karaoke night.

Anyways, a week after Pudderwitz had offered to buy Good Ol' Sal a drink, sure enough they're both back in The Finger Inn; Sal sippin' her soda water and lime, and Pudderwitz scowlin' at her from the bar, barely touchin' his bitter shandy.

It's no good askin' me why he wasn't barred from the place. Do I look like the fuckin' owner to you?

So there he is, one eye fixed on Sal, the other fixed on somethin' else, when suddenly he knocks his drink back in one and makes his way over to the table she's at. Sal glances up from conversation with the ladies; Pudderwitz shoots her his toothiest smile.

"Please, I don't mean to cause trouble. I just wanted to offer my sincerest apologies for last week's *mishap*." Sal forces a smile, accepts his apology, turns back to her friends, and Pudderwitz hovers there for an unhealthy amount o' time, listens to 'em complainin' about the weather, before returnin' to the bar and orderin' another drink. He continues to stare at Sal, only this time his usual smirk has returned.

5

Karaoke night continues without a hitch. First song starts at eight on the dot; some blonde chick gets up and ruins a Dolly Parton number. The audience applaud the final note, not 'cause she's any good, but 'cause they're glad she's fuckin' done. Good Ol' Sal goes up and restores our faith in music, and

Peg Leg Pudderwitz stays at the bar, nursin' his drink, that dirty fuck face o' his locked in place, watchin' Sal sway to the rhythm, her voice spillin' from the speakers like sheets o' soft satin. She finishes the song and smiles as her eyes travel across the room, soaks up the acclaim from her adorin' public. Pudderwitz claps slowly, still smirkin', still starin', and Sal's smile seems to slip slightly as she replaces the microphone and heads back to her table, her eyes kept cautiously on Peg Leg.

Others go up on stage for their three minutes in the spotlight, a lotta 'em too shitfaced to even be able to read the lyrics, end up laughin' their way across the finish line, a little embarrassed no doubt, but not red in the face enough to sit the rest o' the night out. People keep on pesterin' Good Ol' Sal for one more song, and she laughs and says "in a little while," in a way only she knows how to. Peg Leg doesn't move, except this one time when he goes to the men's room. He spends a little longer in there to just be emptyin' the tank, so he was either bangin' out a brown one or scuzzin' into sheets o' double-ply; either way, when he comes out he has this look o' satisfaction on his face, and then he goes right back to the bar and carries on drinkin' his bitter shandy.

A couple o' hours pass before Sal caps the night off with her own take on a Patsy Cline classic. I tell you, the inn went wild. And then Sal just crosses to her table, sips from her glass, has a little laugh and a joke with the ladies. Riley rings the bell, Sal stands, pours the last o' her drink down her throat and reaches for her jacket from the back o' her chair. Pudderwitz has gone from the bar.

Good Ol' Sal has nearly said all her farewells when he suddenly crops up by the entrance. She looks up and sees him, and you could almost see the cogs turnin' in her head, analysin' the situation, figurin' out what to do. She takes a deep breath and heads for the door.

"Good night, Mr. Pudderwitz." She tries to move past him, but he blocks her off.

"How comes I don't get a hug and a kiss?" She looks at him, not sure if he's bein' serious, or if this is his attempt at humour; as a safe bet, Sal wraps her arms around him quick, pulls away before he can take hold, dodges his lips as they race towards her skin.

"I really must be on my way," she says, but still Peg Leg doesn't budge.

"I'm not like these other men. Letting a pretty young thing like you walk these streets at night. And in this weather, too? The winds will blow you right off that bridge! I must insist on accompanying you on your journey." He grabs her arm, and she pulls it away roughly. That's when I happened to step in. Grabbed that peg legged fuck by the collar, pulled his face so close to mine that I could smell his piss breath, and I told him to leave the lady alone. He just smiled at me. "I was just asking the lady if she wanted company on the journey home, that's all. The wind has really picked up tonight, and–"

"I will be fine!" Sal says sternly. Seems Pudderwitz had pissed her off somethin' else. Nobody had heard Sal use that tone o' voice before. She shoves past Pudderwitz, nearly knocks the prick over as she storms out the door and into the night. Peg Leg straightens himself up, and then he looks at me once more with that grin still wide across his face, and he laughs.

I shoulda killed him then and there.

6

Sal was in tears as she fought her way home against the wind. The anger she felt had turned to pain no sooner had she passed Big Joe's, and she was beatin' herself up for lettin' Pudderwitz get to her like that. The wind was stingin' her face, damn near turnin' tear drops into icicles as they slid down her cheeks, forced her to a snail's pace, watched her struggle by the Eight-Til-Late. Word on the street says that Sal was sent to her knees, and stayed down for a good minute before findin' her way back to her feet and takin' the corner onto the shoppin' parade. And she didn't stop again until she was almost on the other side o' the bridge; carefully makes her way across, and then she hears this *knock*in' sound, comin' from behind her. Faint at first, but she stops walkin' so she can listen better, and then each *knock* gets louder than the last.

Who isn't gonna turn around to find out what it is?

So there she is, strainin' her eyes through the dark, holdin' the rope tight as the bridge sways in the wind, and she sees this figure approachin' her. I reckon there was a tiny part o' Sal that was pretty relieved to see it was only Pudderwitz. And a big fuckin' part that was scared shitless.

"What do you want?"

"I told you; I wasn't going to stand by and let the lady walk alone. Not tonight."

"And I told you that I'm fine. Really. There's no need for you to be here."

"Oh, yes there is." He steps closer. *Knock.* "You know, I'm a big fan of that mouth of yours."

"Excuse me?"

"What comes out of it is … truly amazing." *Knock.*

"Well, thank you, I–"

"Why don't we put something amazing *into it* for a change?"

"I don't think I understand–" Pudderwitz pulls out his cock. *Knock.* "You're a disgusting man!"

"Hey, you've seen mine, how about you let me see yours?"

"Stay away." She tries to shuffle backwards, tries to keep her eyes on Pudderwitz, but the wind doesn't make things too easy.

"Come to me." And he starts to play with himself. "Such a pretty voice." Strokin' his prick, getting off on Sal's discomfort. "Let me taste that pussy." She closes her eyes, can't take the sight any longer. "Bring that cunt to me!" Pudderwitz pounces suddenly, and Sal screams as his body connects with hers, knocks her over, lands on top o' her with his hands tearin' at her dress. Sal puts up a struggle, but already Pudderwitz has her wrists pinned down with one hand, while the other makes a grab at her underwear. Sal manages to wrestle an arm free, and strikes Peg Leg across the face. His monocle goes flyin', he screams and hits her back twice as hard. So she's lyin' there next to unconscious, and Peg Leg goes back to smirkin', gives a little laugh as he guides her panties down her thighs and past her knees. Guess he thought it was gonna be that easy.

Guess he underestimated The Bastard Drunk.

7

I knew Pudderwitz wasn't gonna let Good Ol' Sal get home without another encounter, so when I noticed he'd left The Finger Inn, I knocked back the last o' my brandy and made my way towards the bridge. I got there just in time to see that son o' a bitch punch Sal right on the nose. That just made me even angrier, see? So I got over there as fast as I could, I didn't even care that my heavy footsteps might break the damn slats, I just wanted to hurt that sick fuck. He was so engrossed by what he was about to inflict on that poor woman, that he didn't even feel me crossin' the bridge, didn't hear my feet poundin' as I got closer. And then I grab him by the shoulders and throw him backwards. He lands a couple paces away. I crouch down to make sure Good Ol' Sal is still breathin', and that son o' a bitch hits me from behind.

I turn around, and he's standin' there with a knife in his hand, and he slices me just below the eye, blood starts pumpin' out straight away. I drop to my knees, blood is dribblin' down my cheek like there's no tomorrow, and then the fuck puts his shoe against my forehead and pushes me on to my ass. I kick out, miss him, but my boot smashes through that wooden leg o' his and he stumbles, tries to remain upright on uneven limbs, and I get up and I punch him so hard that he drops the knife and lands on his back. He's quick, somehow manages to climb to his foot, tries to come at me again, but I start to pummel him so bad you'd barely recognize that face anymore, wouldn't let him fall down again, held him upright and turned his face into mush. And then I notice that he's still got his cock hangin' out, and I dunno why I did it but I grabbed him so hard down there that I felt his nuts explode, and I loved every second that he screamed.

I shoulda stopped there … but I couldn't. Rage … it had me in a vice, had me in a chokehold, wouldn't let go, and I … I saw the knife lyin' behind Pudderwitz, glistenin' in the moonlight, it was callin' to me, and I … I picked up the knife, and I turned around and he was slidin' along the rope, backin' away from me, beggin', pleadin' me not to do it, and I … I sank it deep into his heart, and Pudderwitz, he … he stepped backwards and … he stepped backwards and his … his splintered leg, it … Good Ol' Sal…

8

Peg Leg Pudderwitz had this look on his face I'd never seen before, not on any man. His eyes were wide, mouth wider, and he just looks at me, tries to say somethin' I'm sure, but he can't find the words. And then just like that he drops sideways, falls from the bridge, and his leg, still stuck inside

Good Ol' Sal's stomach, starts draggin' her down with him. I snapped into life, rushed over and grabbed her body as it was about to slide off the edge, pulled Pudderwitz outta her and watched him disappear into the darkness below. The sound he made when he collided with the tracks is one taken to the grave.

I turn back to Good Ol' Sal; she's still breathin', but she looks as good as dead to me. Next to no colour in her face, and so much blood and guts on display I damn near threw up. She manages to lift her arm, places a weak hand on my cheek, right where Pudderwitz had sliced me.

"My baby," she whispers. I hold her hand, kiss her fingertips, smile through the fuckin' tears.

"You're my baby, too," I tell her. Had been for quite some time. What Emily didn't know wouldn't hurt her, right? But Good Ol' Sal doesn't smile back, she shakes her head; seems I misunderstood what she meant. She guides her hand from my grasp and places it on the gapin' wound in her stomach.

"My baby," she says, and the fuckin' cogs in *my* head, they start turnin', don't they? I look at her, watch silent tears slide down her face and she nods her head. "*Our* baby." I just look at her. It feels like for an age, but I know it couldn't have been more than a few seconds. These voices start shoutin' from the darkness before us. People from the other town, wonderin' what all the noise had been about. Only then does Good Ol' Sal smile. "There might be time," she says, and I can see the pain she is in, and so I do all I can to stop her from hurtin'.

See now, I couldn't let a thing like her pregnancy come to light. What if Emily found out I was the father? It woulda broke her little heart. So before the townsfolk could get any nearer, I rolled Good Ol' Sal off the bridge. Killed her, and anythin' else that mighta still been growin' inside o' her. By the time the first face coulda been seen by moonlight, I was back in Kramusville and on my way back to the Inn.

Riley opened the doors for me, and we sat and I told him everythin' that had happened. He called me every bad name under the sun, and I had no words in which to disagree with him. I was all those things and worse. Once he calmed down, he walked over to the bar and he brought two things back to the table. I nodded.

"Let's make this quick." I pressed the glass o' brandy to my lips and stared into Riley's eyes. I tilted my head back. Before the alcohol had even slid down my throat, the bullet smacked into my beatin' heart.

And boys, I think I just divulged you with a little too much information.

The Legacy

The Bastard Drunk suddenly had a sobered expression on his face. His eyebrows narrowed as he cast a sincere gaze upon the travellers, who were stunned into a silence, which Fitz chose to break after a short while with an abrupt snort.

"You've told us some shit tonight, Bastard, but that one takes the crown." He stood up and grabbed his coat from the back of the chair. "You weren't wrong; the night ends here. What a waste of my time. Come on Paul, our train will be here soon."

"But the voices I heard at the bridge," Paul replied, almost in a trance. "Those were the exact words, Fitz. There's no other explanation; he was telling the truth."

"About Pudderwitz, maybe! But we've been sat right in front of that piece of shit for the best part of eight fucking hours; how do you explain that if he's dead?" The Bastard slowly got to his feet, and pulled open his coat. Beneath it, he wore a pale blue shirt, on which there was a small hole surrounded by dried claret; The Bastard lifted the shirt to display a blood stained wound in his chest. Even Fitz gulped at the sight of the torn flesh. And then, to his and Paul's horror, The Bastard plunged a thumb and finger inside, his face emotionless as his digits slurped around before producing a bullet, which he allowed to drop to the table with a thud.

Fitz let out an anguished groan, while Paul vomited hard at his feet. Shaking, wiping bile from the corners of his mouth, he pointed a wavering finger at The Bastard.

"How–"

"Same way Polly still answers phones at The Millerbank. Same way Peg Leg and Sal still argue on the bridge. Same way them fuckin' zombie kids still load grocery bags o' Lucille into the boot o' her car. You honestly didn't see this comin'? The signs were there, boys. I said it once already; I live and die at The Finger Inn."

"Let's get the fuck out of here," Fitz cried.

"You don't think we can jus' let ya walk outta here alive after what you've jus' heard, do you?" Riley placed two pints of ale on the table. The travellers just had time to look at him as he pulled a gun from his belt and placed it next to the glasses. "Drink up, fellas," he croaked with a toothless smile. With great haste, Fitz snatched the firearm up into his grasp and aimed it at the barman, at The Bastard, back to the barman. The Bastard just laughed.

"And what good is a livin' finger around a trigger if it shoots bullets only at the dead?" Riley made a move closer towards them, and in a panic Fitz fired off two shots into the barman's stomach. As the echoes of the gun subsided into silence, the travellers watched with terror as Riley unbuttoned his shirt to reveal not a single bullet wound, but grotesque burns all over his skin. He raised a hand to the hair on his head, and pulled it off without a care in the world, allowed the toupee to fall at his feet. Finally, he removed the gloves from what were his hands; crisp and blackened, almost unrecognizable as those that had served drinks all evening. Fitz dropped the weapon in fear and retreated against the wall.

"You..." he stammered weakly. "You're ... You can't be."

"Oh, I am," the barman replied. "Whether you choose to believe it or not, ain't no blood coursin' through these veins o' mine."

"You're dead," Fitz whispered, and he repeated it quietly to himself, as though willing himself to believe what was before his eyes. "You're dead."

"Correct," The Bastard said, rising. "You've been right about a couple o' other things, too." He pulled an envelope and a letter opener from an inside pocket of his coat and looked at Paul. "You must've dropped this earlier. Carol's a good woman, keepin' you in the loop like this. I can't imagine why you wouldn't wanna see the photographs o' your son, Paul. He's got his father's eyes." He dropped the envelope to the table; Paul instantly recognized the white cover, and his name in black handwriting on the front. Through the thin slit The Bastard had created in the top, a photograph slid partially into view, of a young boy posing in his school uniform. Silent tears streamed down Paul's cheeks as he placed a hand upon his only child's face.

"You son of a bitch," he spat softly. "You had no right. No fucking right! Do you get off on other people's misery, is that it? Does it make you feel more of a man?" The Bastard just shook his head.

"No, sir. No, I do not. In fact, if I had breath to expel from my lungs, I might even sigh in exasperation at the thought o' another lonely child in this world. But you see, I don't breathe, and I don't bleed, and I don't feel. 'Cause the dead, we feel nothin'; ain't that the truth, Fitz? And the livin'? They feel every fuckin' thing." In an instant, The Bastard slammed his fist down on the table. Paul snatched his hand away as fast as he could, but as he staggered back, he stared down at the letter opener speared through his son's face. Anger surged through his body, quickly replaced by a burning agony; at first, he was sure the pain came from the ruined photograph. But then he noticed the finger lying inches from his envelope. Paul hesitantly looked down at his hand; and saw nothing in place of his middle digit. Blood spurted into the void above his knuckle, visible beyond a jagged flap of flesh, and the man screamed as though no man had ever screamed before. He dropped to his knees and clutched his other hand around his wrist, as though to stem the flow of blood, but to no avail. Fitz's face had turned a paler shade of white as he looked at his friend's severed finger.

"We're going to die."

"Everybody dies in the end, Mr. Muscle Man," Riley mused. "Jus' be thankful that you lived this long." There was the sudden sound of creaking wood, as delicate feet padded on the fragile floorboards overhead. "Right on cue." The barman smiled. "Time for you boys to meet my own baby."

"Daddy?" A voice so soft and gentle, slicing through the atmosphere with little effort, drew closer as footsteps descended a staircase and headed towards them. The curtain behind the bar twitched; and from beyond appeared a young girl the travellers instantly recognized. Her honey coloured eyes stared out from beneath a bedraggled mass of fierce black hair, which framed a badly disfigured face. Her rags barely concealed a frail and broken body, and as she exchanged glances with two strangers, she nervously twisted the remains of a head upon a doll's distorted body. "Daddy, I heard the screams again. Who are these men?"

"Peyton." Paul blurted the girl's name out so strongly, that the fact he even knew her name at all startled her more than it otherwise would have. "Peyton, come here."

"Daddy—" Her face appeared frightened, as she looked to Riley for comfort, but Paul continued.

"Come here, sweetheart, everything's going to be okay, he can't hurt you anymore."

"Paul, it's too late," Fitz said.

"What do they mean?" the girl cried. "Daddy—"

"He's not your real father! Come with me."

"Hold your tongue!" Riley growled fiercely.

"You're no father, you're a fucking paedophile!"

"Paul, it's too late!"

"Watch your mouth!"

"Daddy, what are they saying?"

"Paul, she's dead! Peyton's dead, they're all fucking dead!" Fitz's roar ended the cacophony of sound, aside from the hearty sobs escaping from the poor girl, who turned and ran. Her footsteps sounded heavily up the staircase and overhead, before ceasing altogether. Riley turned his attention from the curtain to Paul and Fitz. He glared at the travellers. He stepped so steadily forward. He picked up the gun.

"What are you going to do?" Fitz asked fearfully. Riley continued to hold his gaze.

"You upset my daughter; I upset you." Without a single fleck of emotion, he aimed the gun at Paul and held a withered finger against the trigger. The shot sounded. Candle lights flickered as a bullet exploded from the barrel and screamed through the air towards Paul's face. What happened in less than a second seemed like an eternity, as Fitz watched his friend recoil wickedly on impact. His glasses spun from his face, as the tiny lead projectile pierced the right lens. Smacked into his eye, tore deep through his brain, exploded from the back of his head. Blood and brain decorated the walls as the life within faded fast; and then his body came to a sickening still on the wooden floor.

"No!" Fitz cried, rushing to cradle his friend, trying to will him back to life, but only succeeding in turning himself into a bloody mess, as claret spilled from the gaping hole in Paul's head and turned Fitz's white top into a sticky red canvas. Riley scratched his head with the tip of the firearm.

"My aim is definitely not improvin'," he said to The Bastard. "I'll get me another heart shot one day."

"Makes a change for you to shoot anybody these days," The Bastard replied. "Since the mess you made o' killin' those exchange students, I thought you preferred to use a blade."

"I don't have a preference, Hanson; as long as they die, it doesn't matter, does it?"

"Course it fuckin' matters! How many times have you heard me say it? You come to know enough about someone, you start to care; only then is the time right for me to kill 'em off in spectacular fashion." The barman snorted as he handed the gun to The Bastard.

"Funny how you feel for your audience, an' yet feel nothin' at all."

"I wouldn't expect you to understand. You're not a storyteller like me, Riley; you're just a character in one o' my tales." The Bastard aimed the gun at Fitz; the traveller slowly turned to face him.

"Everything's a fucking script to you, isn't it? Every word, every action. I bet even the little arguments you've had are tried and tested; little plot devices in the same fucking story you live time and time again. What the fuck do you gain from all of this?"

"Gina's army saw our once great community diminish. Those who could afford to, moved away in a heartbeat; and those who couldn't were forced to brave the voices on the wind. Kramusville became somethin' o' a wounded animal; and then a dead child molester workin' the local pub killed it off once and for all. You chase a man and watch him die in a fire one minute, you don't expect him to be fillin' your glass the next. They knew they couldn't hurt Riley any more, but he could hurt them; so by any means necessary they upped and left too. We're just tryna make things right by repopulatin' the place we love so much, is all. It can get pretty lonely here in the afterlife. We always appreciate the company really. Your friend said it himself; this is a ghost town. And he's our newest resident."

"You son of a bitch. You think you're the fucking hero in all of this? What a gift to the world! This whole night has been a formality, hasn't it? As soon as we walked through those doors, you knew you were going to kill us, didn't you?"

The Bastard shook his head.

"I knew I was gonna kill you the moment I walked past you on the bridge."

You'll die by my hand tonight.

"I didn't–"

"We *choose* to reveal ourselves, only when the time is right." And all at once, Fitz saw it. The brunette woman in a bloodied white dress stood by the stage, a gaping hole in her stomach, sobbing quietly into a glass of soda water and lime. The badly bruised gentleman with the broken wooden leg at the bar, nursing what remained of his genitals. The chubby, legless teen, deep in silent discussion with his blonde haired friend, who toyed aimlessly with the thin wooden stick jutting from his eye. The smartly dressed young lady, her face a beaten pulp, staring up at the empty space between her shoulders, from the head resting upon her lap. Something tapped against Fitz's foot.

"My glasses…" The traveller backed into the wall and looked on with sheer fright as Paul searched aimlessly for his spectacles, found them, pressed them to his face. "At least they'll know where to look for our bodies; right, Fitz?" Without another moment's hesitation, Fitz turned and ran for the exit. The door was as stiff as he could recall, but with a great heave he tore it open, immediately bathed in the light of morning. The sun was fierce, and he almost recoiled, though the thought of The Bastard's gun urged him on.

A man was walking his dog across the street. The sound of the inn door thudding shut alerted him. He stopped suddenly, his head slowly turning in the inn's direction. Fitz shielded the sunlight from his eyes, and saw a gaping hole where the man's mouth should've been. Bloodstains littered an otherwise pale blue polo shirt, splashes of red upon a badge, concealing the name it bore, though Fitz was certain he knew him. The man dropped the leash he had clutched in his right hand, and the dog bounded over to Fitz, sank its teeth into his jeans, and Fitz froze at the sight of the bitch's burnt coat and ravaged skin. A tooth scraped across Fitz's leg, and he yelled as he kicked the whimpering mutt away. There was the sound of an approaching train. The man pulled out a gun and fired at Fitz; the bullet whistled past his ear and pinged against a drainpipe. Fitz began running towards the train station. An old man was stood before him, gazing aimlessly up to the sky, the gash in his neck slurped open.

As the traveller neared, the old man made a grab for him, and their bodies collided.

Fitz's notebook fell to the floor as the old man spun into the ticket booth, in which a middle aged woman sat, her eyes rolled into the top of her head, saliva foaming from her twisted mouth. The traveller stole a glance back as he descended the stairs to the platform; another bullet flew past him as the dog rushed excitedly towards the station. Fitz darted inside the train, and the doors gradually ground to a close. The dog barked furiously on the other side of the glass; and then it faded away before Fitz's very eyes, until he was no longer staring down in exasperation at a dead dog, but just a tattered slab of concrete. Fitz dropped into the nearest seat, as the train jerked into life and exited St. Arthur's Walk.

And just as suddenly as they'd all appeared, they vanished. The street once again appeared as barren as the night before; and The Finger Inn, a deserted public house, aside from a dead body, a barman, and The Bastard Drunk. Riley looked in disbelief at Hanson, who was still aiming his weapon at the doorway.

"Why'd you let that one get away?" Riley asked. The Bastard exhaled deeply.

"Somethin' he said struck a chord. Everybody wants to leave a legacy, Riley; a real gift to the world. Mine was growin' inside o' the woman I loved, only to die before it ever got to see the light o' day. That boy has given me a second chance." The Bastard lowered the gun to his side. His eyes fell on to Paul. "Bag this body up, take him to Courtenay Grimper's house. Remember, the combination is 31013. At the very least we'll have another tale to tell next time."

"An' the finger?" The Bastard sported a wry grin.

"Put it in a jar behind the bar; I think this place just inherited a legacy too." Riley smiled as he took the digit into his hand and walked to the bar, only to return seconds later with a mop and a large black duffel bag. The Bastard picked up a glass of ale, pinched his eyes shut tight and took a long, hard sip. He let out hoarse approval, and licked his lips in satisfaction.

"There was a time when I thought that was it. That the name Hanson Hutchison meant nothin' to anyone any more, and that was the end. But no longer." Riley peeled his eyes away from the duffel bag to glance up at him. "Mr. Fitz won't make it to The Millerbank Hotel, we both know that. He'll meet a fate akin to Pretty Polly; no one needs to hear the same story twice. But someone will come lookin' for these boys. Someone will find that notebook, and someone will commit my words to paper. Kramusville will be back on the map, my friend. And sooner or later, everyone will know the tales o' The Bastard Drunk."

Special Thanks

First of all, to my guinea pigs; Dane and Janie, for proofreading an early draft, and Michael, for providing detailed and humorous feedback.

To UEL class of 2012; particularly Helena, Tessa and Tim, for their dedication and guidance, and Sally, for the insight into a novelist's mind.

Lastly, I would like to thank my family for their amazing support, and for not seeking medical advice every time I pitched a new idea.

www.dmwoon.wordpress.com

Printed in Great Britain
by Amazon.co.uk, Ltd.,
Marston Gate.